EVERYBODY WANTS HER

EVERYBODY WANTS HER

By B'Shone

Published by
MIDNIGHT EXPRESS BOOKS

EVERYBODY WANTS HER

Published by
MIDNIGHT EXPRESS BOOKS
POBox 69
Berryville AR 72616
(870) 210-3772
MEBooks1@yahoo.com

Artword by Quintell Wilson
INMARK DESIGNS
(901) 308-4994

EVERYBODY WANTS HER

By B'Shone

ACKNOWLEDGEMENTS

To God Almighty for loving me so much! Without him there would be no me. All praises goes to him for allowing me to go through my life experiences and come out victorious.

Also to Victor and Linda Huddleston at Midnight Express for taking the time out to oversee this project; thank you guys very much.

Margaret, Luther Sr., Moneeka, Shuntell, Lukina(aka) Squirt, Lil Luke, Lil Travis, Kylan, and Miesha. Love you all.

Rest in Peace "Laura Mae Rowand". Miss you, granny.

"Joe JT Taylor" Miss you brother.

My loyal characters" Greg "G-Ink" Green, Shaw, Lawrence 'Big O' Odom, Alex 'Lil Dillin' Dillard, Mr. Ward, Winbush, J. McDaniel, Bobo Bates, C. Jackson, R. Garland, Malcolm Gopher, Randy 'Big Runn' Harris, Courtney 'Fame' Smith, Cassell Brown, Jack Williams Jr., Joe aka Scoota. Thank you all for your support.

CHAPTER 1 The Book Signing

"I want everyone!" the Commentator shouted, "to get up out of your seat and give a warm round of applause to the Essence Best Selling author of 'She Made me Cheat, and...'" before she could finish introducing the guest speaker, applause, cheers, and screams filled the auditorium. "And, the Evil Within She! Give it up for my girl, Moneeka Folks!"

Slowly, but seductively, Moneeka gracefully walked across the stage as straight man and gay woman gawked at one of the sexiest body they had ever seen. The colorful lights glistened off her cocoa-brown skin that shined so radiantly. The 5'7" beauty was definitely a show stopper.

Moneeka could not help the way her peach and cream body dress clung to her curvaceous hips, bringing much unwanted attention to her perfectly round back side. With every step she took, her butt cheeks moved up and down like two small volleyballs. Her perky D-cups sat just right on her body frame as if to be two coconuts, ready to be tasted. Moneeka silky black hair swayed from side to side, bouncing with every motion of her head.

She stepped to the podium, gently placed the loose hair behind her ear.

A tall slender white male leaned over to his female friend and said, "Tess, I tell you the truth. I'll drink that girl bath water, and be waiting on her to do it again." Tess being a dyke, smiled at the comment. Tess tongue grazed across the bottom portion of her lip, as her right hand discreetly went between her thighs, felling her warmth.

Softly Tess moaned, "Boy, if you only knew what I was thinking."

At that moment: the applause ended, and everyone took their seats. Moneeka stood there smiling at the audience.

"First I would like to thank every one of you for coming out in support of my new book and the continuing support for my previous two." She spoke with such poise, as if to be a college professor.

She placed the manuscript on the podium, then opened it. "I would like to read to you a couple of paragraphs in my new book, 'Everybody Wants Her'."

Tess mouthed, "I want you too." but no vocals came out, as she squirmed in her seat. Moneeka continued to smile, as she began to read.

"Robin walks in her home to the sound of sex noises coming from her master bed room. She paused. Quickly taking off her six inch high heel, Jimmy Choo, shoes to prevent any clacking on her hardwood floors. Slowly, she made it to her bedroom, only to find her husband in their bed with her. Could it be? Fueled with rage and surprise, she angrily stood at the door and observed their actions.

It was her. Micole Perison. A high class, high maintenance female that used her body only to get a baller, but never give up the booty!

If your pocket wasn't deep, you didn't have a mansion on the hills, or drove what Lloyd Banks, said "Beamer, Benz, or Bentley," her time you got none of, and don't even think about the sex. But somehow, Robin's husband Shone mange to get it and get it he was.

"Micole moans out of pure ecstasy. Her head hung off the bed as to hit the floor, with her eyes closed. Her red finger nails dug into Shone's bald head. Her legs where wrapped around his neck while he orally pleased her."

"Uummm, tastes like candy," Shone said as he came up for air.

"Robin continued to observe from the door. She pondered over how could her husband get Micole? Not the fact that he was getting ready to insert his penis in her wetness, but it was with her, But how? As her eyes continued to stay focus on the two she was getting turned on by Micole's flawless body. Micole didn't have a mark on her. Her natural beauty was stunning and enticing."

"Robin reached behind her back and unzips her long black skirt allowing it to drop to the floor, as she quickly took off her black thong and tossed it into the room next to Micole's head. Still in the heat of the moment they never notice her standing there. Again she watched her husband penned Micole's legs against the headboard, as he inserted all nine inches of his large penis in Micole's neatly shaved vagina."

Low moans, and groans echoed threw out the auditorium, as

Moneeka continued reading.

Shone bit down on his lips and sped up his stroke. In and out. Slow and fast. Hard and soft. He pounded Micole again and again as she cried out in passion.

Robin took her middle finger and played with her clitoris while watching her own live porn show. The louder Micole got the wetter Robin became.

Tess had forgotten that she was at a large book signing, and sitting on the front row of the auditorium. She let her head rest on the back of the chair, closed her eyes, and placed her right hand into her sweat pants, and commenced to massaging her clitoris, and breathing heavy. Her male friend glanced over at her and watched.

Needless to say, the guest speaker Moneeka noticed and quickly took a lengthy stare at Tess without breaking her stride in reading. Moneeka had a tingling sensation shoot threw her body while at the podium. "Oh my," she said to herself, realizing that she had just came in her thong. She crossed her legs and sped up the reading. Her seductive tone was now gone.

"Robin began to climax. Micole's body trembled, as Shone pulled out of her wetness, and shot..." Moneeka stopped there. She looked out at the audience and noticed that everyone was on the edge of their seats. Some with their eyes closed, some with their hands in their pants, and others watching her with their mouth gapped open.

Standing behind the wooden podium, Moneeka discreetly wiped between her legs. She had come also, but not like the others. She had climaxed by watching Tess massage her kitty kat. Again her sexy tone returned.

"I'm going to stop right here. Woo... it was getting hot in that bed room. So please finish reading it, and email me at Moneekafire@yahoo.com. I can see everyone was paying close attention. But that's good, right?"

"Yes!" the crowd yelled.

Moneeka forced a smile on her face. She wanted badly to get off the stage to go clean herself up and take a long shower.

Screams and applause-filled the room.

"I would like to thank you all for coming out to support me again, and I promise to keep nothing but the best for my fans to read. Let's make this another best seller. I love you! Goodnight." Some of the fellows called out her name, but she wasted no time leaving the stage, she stared at Tess as she made her exit.

Again her body shivered, as with a majestic tough. Moneeka gave a friendly wave and exit the stage. Tresha the commentator stood on the side of the stage waiting for her.

"Girl that chapter got me horny as hell!" she stressed. "I don't have a man right now, but whomever I put this on." Tresha patted her private. "I'ma put it on him; make 'em wanna marry me."

They both laughed.

"Girl, how did you come up with that story? Was it real? Cause girl it was like I was there."

Moneeka smiled, "Hell," her sexy tone had disappeared again. She now talked like a white nerd, although she's black. "Gee, oh my. I felt like I was getting rammed while I was on the stage. Girl, I came all over myself. Did you see that girl in the front row?"

"What girl?" Tresha asked.

"Never mind."

CHAPTER 2 Club Flirt

Music blasting, hoochies shaking, playa's playing, and haters preying. The party was jumping at Club Flirt, the only hot spot in the city that had the best mix crowd around Memphis, Tennessee.

"We're live at Club Flirt, the 250O block of Winchester; where the old, Club Tiffany, use to be!" DJ Jay-Mac yelled on the microphone.

"The place to be, where it all goes down! Head bobbing, booty shaking, and money making!" He continued to scream out, as he held a pair of Beats by Dre head phones to his right ear, while mixing Yo Gotti, 5 Star Chick before blazing the mic again.

"Uuup-oooh, there they go! It's King Tydizzle and the T.B.F. crew just entered the building! Ladies, and ya' fake balla's get ready to see how real balla's ball! Wat up boy?!"

King and his crew headed straight for the second level V.I.P. section as Lil Dillin, and King's baby brother, Big O, escorted some bad chicks to the V.I.P along with them.

Lil Dillin sipping on a bottle of Moet, "This joint packed to capacity!" screaming over the loud music. "Nut'n but wall-to-wall pussy! Just look!" he pointed out to the crowd.

King looked at Lil Dillin shaking his head, "Calm down, D! You still act like the same lil nigga that always kept me in trouble when we were doing our FED bid!"

Big O chimed in, "Big Bruh, we some made nigga now, fuck what ya talkin' 'bout!" Big O, told his oldest brother, with a young lady bouncing up and down on his lap. King continued to stand by the window looking out into the club, and that's when he saw her. A thick, coco skin, Serna Williams body having woman walked throw the door. Her hips swayed from side to side, having every man's attention she passes. Her black hip hugger jeans were so tight that they appeared to be' painted on her body. Her cream and black body blouse told the story of her breast. Just right. As she tried to make her way toward the bar, every man in the club tugged on her and her girlfriend.

King stared at her as if he had found his future wife. "Yeah, that's her." he mumbled to himself."

Big O noticed, that he said something, "What you say?" He screamed, as King visual were locked on the mystery woman. Moments later, Lil Dillin stood and walked over to the window to observe what King was looking at, with another bottle of Moet in hand.

Lil Dillin glared out in the crowd and found her, "I be damn! That freak is fine!" he yelled, looking at her back side from afar. Finally,

DJ Jay Mac recognized her face.

"Oh yes!" Jay Mac yelled, "It's her! The Queen of Urban novels! The Essence's best seller is in the club! What's up, Moneeka?" She turned, waved and gave him a warm Friday night smile.

"Holla at cha boy before you get up outta here." She nodded in agreement at Jay Mac.

"Oh snap! That is that chick who writes those freaky books! I know she be writing 'bout herself!" Lil Dillin said, excitedly.

Quickly Big O tossed the slim chick out of his lap and rushed over to the window, looking down. "Where she at? Oh neva' mind. I see her. I've read all her books, and jacked off to most of them!"

King and Lil Dillin looked on in disgust, but said nothing. King stood there in a daze. He took it upon himself to go down and make her acquaintance.

"Come on." said King.

They exited and headed in the direction of the lower section of the club, but not before bumping into Alabama Malcolm. A tall, blacker than train smoke, drug dealer that fought with King over the 1300 block of Hyde Park. That was then, this is now King gave up the street life and started producing movies and he also had a very lucrative construction company that made well over ten million in profit a year.

Malcolm thought that he had won the war. He bragged to his crew that he forced King to retire, and to get away from the 1300 block; that is, until King and his crew caught Malcolm slipping, and put them choppers in his mouth.

"Let's just do him right here!" Big O suggested. King said nothing.

"Nigga you lying like you ran us off?" Lil Dillin agitated.

Malcolm nervously stated, "Hold up. King it ain't like that. But if this is what it's gonna be, get it ova with." Malcolm wasn't a coward; however, he didn't want beef with King either. King was known for laying a sucker down, back in his heyday. They could have killed him easily, but King just wanted him to know that he can reach out and touch him up anytime he got ready.

"Let him go." Malcolm walked off, but not before stopping him, "Leave well enough alone." King said.

Although, Malcolm walked away unharmed, he didn't like the fact that King caught him coming out of his trap house without his goon squad.

He had to get revenge.

King stopped in front of Malcolm, "What's up?" Malcolm asked, not with beef, but more out of respect.

"Shit." King said, nonchalantly. "We good?"

Malcolm smiled, "Fo sho." They both nodded, and kept it moving.

Moneeka and her girl friend stopped at the bar and got something to drink before entering the Lower Level V.I.P. She observed King and his crew as they walked in her direction.

"Oh my gosh! I can't go anywhere and have a freakin' good time without some wanna be thug, coming up to me...trying to run a pimp line on me, or quoting something from my book. They all think because I write freaky books that I'm a freak!"Moneeka shouted over the music to her friend Angie.

Her Beverly Hills 90210 accent had Angie laughing.

"Girl, I'ma find you a black ass hood nigga, to put some big black wood up in your wanna be white ass! Just so he can find your lost soul!" Angie continued to laugh. "And plus, this is the life you chose!"

"Here come some more of them fake thugs." Moneeka said, "Let me put on my fake smile. Who knows, they might buy a sister's book." placing a wide smile on her face, as King got closer, Moneeka was prepared to converse with him; however, he decided not to. He chose the latter, and walked right pass her. To Moneeka surprise, it shocked the hell out of her. She was so used to men wanting her number, or autograph that it bothered her. She swiveled in her seat taking a strange look at the back of King's head. Angie notice how Moneeka's mouth was gasping open. She knew first hand that Moneeka thought too highly of herself.

"About time. He just made my night." Moneeka lied, "I truly did not feel like being bothered with all his lies about how much money he got, or the car he drives."

"Bitch, stop lying and pick ya' bottom lip up off the dance flo'. That nigga hurt ya' feelings like a mutha!"Angie laughed.

Moneeka got up and headed for the rest room. "I'll be back!" forcefully, Moneeka said.

As she entered the ladies room, and noticed how clean it was she stood in front of the mirror and reapplied her makeup. Silently, she talked to herself, until she heard some moaning sounds coming from around the corner of the restroom. Thinking that some one was hurt she slowly turned the corner only to find two gay females eating one another's wetness. They never noticed her standing a few feet away from them watching everything unfold. Moneeka stood there and watched not because she was interested in joining, but it was something she could place in her next novel.

She watched as the girl with her eyes close head rolled in a circular motion while sitting in a chair with her hand on the back of another girl's head, guiding her every movement. Pleasure one was giving, and a joyful feeling the other received.

That's when Moneeka gasped for air, making herself known. The two ladies looked up seeing Moneeka standing there. One smiled, and the other panicked. It was her, the woman that made Moneeka cum on herself in public, and was about to make her do it again.

"Join us." Tess said, but Moneeka stood still. Without delay, Tess buried her head back into the slender white female's hot love oven. All the while eyeing Moneeka. Discreetly she rubbed her breast, then the warmth between her thighs. Moneeka was turned on. She was about to take her clothes off until someone entered the rest room. Angie. Quickly she turned and headed for the door.

"Girl, what's taking you so long?"

"I had to use it." Moneeka said, as she forced Angie out of the ladies room. "And redo my make up."

In the lower level V.I.P, among the celebrities were 8 Ball, MJG,

Yo Gotti, and Nasty Nardo. King and his crew mix & mingled with the best of them, as all the groupies danced on top of tables, and them. Moneeka and Angie entered, and took a seat. Yo Gotti got upon Angie and MJG spoke to Moneeka, however her eyes were still glued on King. An hour later King and his crew headed for the door. Trialing close behind them was Moneeka and Angie. They too were preparing to leave.

As they all reached the exit, Lil Dillin whom was intoxicated turned to Moneeka, and asked, "What's up?" He slurred his words, "You wanna fuck with me or what?"

Quickly she frowned and turned her nose up, "Excuse you?"

"Neva' mind him. He's fucked up!" Big O said, laughing.

"Fuck her then," he turned to Angie, "Hell what 'bout you? You look betta anyway." Lil Dillin was wasted. King and Big O took him by the arms and escorted him out of the club. Again, Kings said nothing to Moneeka.

They walked out into the parking lot only to find it pack with every hoochie in the city fighting for attention with, too small boy shorts on, miniskirts, Daisy Duke, and skin tight jeans, all car hopping, looking for a baller for the night. Whoever, drove a Beam, Benz, or Bentley got the booty.

King headed to his all black CL550, was approached by one of his old workers, Big Runn "What it do, King?" Runn, asked. Before King said a word, he spotted Moneeka slowly walking his way. He asked Big Runn.

13

"Which car you driving tonight?"

Runn pointed, "My blue, four-door Cut-dawg." Runn's 85 Cutlass was sitting on chrome 22's, right next to Moneeka's 755 Beamer. "Why? You gud?"

"Yeah, take my Benz, and I'll take your car, and get mine in the morning." King said.

"That's what's up." Big Runn tossed his keys to King, and they departed.

King was preparing to get in the vehicle, however, before he could Moneeka walked by being sarcastic. "Nice car." They giggled as she got in her Beamer. King got in the Cutlass and started the engine. He noticed that Moneeka was trying to get his attention. Her window came down as her arm waved out of it. He glanced to the right and let his passenger side window down. She tried to flirt, but he ignored her.

"Would you like to call me?"Moneeka asked.

King smiled, put his car in reverse and backed out, not saying a word.

Again, Angie laughed. "Girl, you too funny. This is the second time tonight he walked pass you...wait this time he drove away from ya' ass! Woo...I told you, you ain't all that!" Angie continued to laugh the entire ride home. Moneeka was thrown aback. Angie saw it written all over her face. Embarrassed.

CHAPTER 3 They Meet

"What time we're leaving?" Angie asked, Moneeka, "And where we going again?" She asked loudly, placing her phone on loud speaker as she tossed it on her bed, and continued to pack.

"Our flight leaves at 3:30pm; so make sure you're on time!" Moneeka strongly stated, "And we're heading to the A.T.L."

"I'll be there just as soon as," Angie's voice changed to sultry, while licking her full grown water melon lips. Her tongue came out of her mouth, and hung over her bottom lip, like water diving off the cliff. "Virginia BoBo, makes it over here and changes my oil, and gives me a tune-up."

"Oh my gosh, Angie, you still sleeping with him? He hasn't asked you to marry him yet! Why, you giving up the booty?"Moneeka asked.

"Girl, that tall glass of wine taste gud as a mutha in my mouth, and plus," Angie said, again allowing her tongue to slip in and out of her mouth, as she stepped out of her sweat pants, preparing to jump into the shower, "plus, that boy can eat some, pu..."

"Angie, that's 'TMI'," Moneeka interrupted her. "Just be here on time!" She shouted as she hung up the phone.

Angie stood in the mirror admiring her small, but petite, body. She was built like the sexy Kelly Rowland. Angie was 5'2", hazel eyes, caramel skin tone and ghetto fabulous. Her sex appeal and attitude was enough to make any man happy to have as his ride or die chick. Better yet, if he was serious about life she was definitely wifey material. If she was in a relationship with you, she stayed down to the very end. No-one could tell her anything about the one she loved. However, Angie's reputation was jacked up. Several, cats from the hood lied like she was a whore that slept around with any and everybody. When the truth was, they never got the booty. Truth is she would only spread her legs for the one she thought loved her. Her man.

Angie was only looking for the love she never received from her father, who abandoned her and her mother when her mother suffered from throat cancer. He found a rich older white woman. Angie was 14 years old and she never got that affection that she so desired from a man. She never forgave her sperm donor. After she graduated from high school, her mother passed away.

Angie now 27, had yearned for that love again, but never had received it. She longed for her motherly love so much that she went out searching for false love. Many times she was deceived by several men claiming that they loved her, but only wanted her body. Angie even started dancing in the strip clubs in search for something, but couldn't find it. After-so many years of nothing, she vowed to protect her heart from predators that preyed on her vulnerability. That is until she met BoBo. This tall 6'2" light bright, damn near white brother with dreads that hung down his back had stolen her heart. He was kind, caring, and loving to her. The love she always wanted, had finally found her.

BoBo was from Richmond, Virginia, but was a New York Knicks fan, that's how Angie met him. By her being a Memphis Grizzle's fan, her and Moneeka attended the Grizzle's vs Knicks game. In the mist of them enjoying the Grizzle's victory over the Knicks, BoBo introduced himself, at the concession stand..

After a few months of dating, he moved to Memphis. Angie knew that he was into Real -Estate and informed him of how much cheaper the housing market is, and how he could build his empire in a smaller market, with her help. Although, he had his own place, the two was most definitely dating they had keys to each other's homes.

Angie continued to prance around her room naked dancing to 'Jay Z's On to the Next One' there was a knock at her door.

"Damn, who is this?" She asked herself, while looking at the time.

"10 o'clock. That can't be, my baby. He said he'll be here at eleven."

Angie grabbed her sexy red lace bath robe, and tossed it over her sculptured body and rushed to the door, screaming, "Who is it?" She waited to hear someone, but got no response. She stood on her tip toes and looked through the peep hole only to see her long time friend. Quickly, she opened the door.

"Awww...bitch get in her!" Angie yelled out. "Where have you been?" She said inviting her girlfriend into her home. Angie had forgotten just that fast that she wasn't wearing anything underneath her lace bathrobe as her arms flew open to embarrass her.

"Damn girl!" her friend shouted, looking at Angie's perfect body over, as Angie's nipples got hard due to the cool breeze that rushed through the house, but so did her girlfriend eyes. "Ang, ya' ass is still as fine as they come." She looked Angie up and down. "I sho' wish you were into women, because I would eat that pussy up! Mmmmuummm..." her friend licked her lips, as she cooed at Angie. "Give me another hug?" she asked stepping closed to Angie, however, Angie stepped back quickly.

"A'ight bitch! Don't play." Angie said, playfully rolling her eyes. "And you of all people know me, Tess. It's strickly dickly with me. My man can eat pussy betta than any woman can."

"Stop lying, Ang. There's no man walking on God's green earth that can eat, or touch a woman in every spot she needs to be licked or touched like a woman." Tess proclaimed.

"Anyway, how long have you been in, Memphis Tennessee?"

"Bout a week or so. I been job hunting," Tess paused and gave Angie an evil smirk, "You know, just doing my thang."

Angie walked toward her bed room, as Tess followed close behind, getting a bird's eye view of that soft, round back side, that wiggled with every step she took. Tess wanted her badly.

Tess and Angie met at Pure Passion Gentlemen Club, where Angie danced after her mother passed away. It wasn't something she enjoyed, but needless to say, it paid her bills. Tess being a madam-Female Pimp- had came to Memphis along with a couple of her whores in search for some new recruits, and notice a stressful disposition on Angie's face as she sat in the club watching her girls turn tricks. Tess took it upon herself to converse with Angie. After finding out her life story she decided to take her under her wings. Not to be pimped, but to teach her the street life and how to fend for self. By using what she got to survive in this manly world. Angie never forgot about her, but somehow their connection dissipated.

"Ang, you getting ready to go somewhere?" Tess asked, after noticing all the clothes scattered across the bed, and the luggage on the floor.

"Yeah, me and my girl is heading to the A at 3:30." Angie shouted, from her bathroom, as the shower water ran.

"Okay. So, when are you coming back?" She asked, as she begun looking threw Angie's drawers as to be searching for something lost. Before Angie could answer there was a knock at the door.

"Someone's at the door. Want me to get it?" she screamed at Angie.

Tess didn't wait for Angie to answer her. She hustled to the door screaming out, "Who is it?"

There he stood smiling. BoBo. Tess opened the door.

"Hey ba...by." BoBo was thrown aback by the strange woman at the door. He had never known Angie to have any company, but Moneeka. BoBo walked into the house without saying a word to her. Tess took it upon herself to extend her hand to greet him.

"Hi, I'm Tess, and you are?"

19

"A hard dick, looking for my pussy. Where is it?"

Seductively Tess cooed, "Umm, she's in the shower." Tess looked him up and down, noticing the bulge that came from his tan dress slacks.

BoBo walked off heading directly toward his woman. He stood in the rest room not saying anything as he got undressed, leaving the door open, as he noticed Tess observing his every move. He could have cared less, he only wanted Angie. He got in the shower and whispered in her ear.

"Daddy's here."

Angie immediately turned around and begun to tongue wrestle with her love. Slowly Angie made her way down to his chisel chest, where BoBo looked down at her. Angie decided to go a little further, and made it to his rock hard six pack, as her tongue traced every ab on his stomach.

Finally, she had reached his eight inch pole of love.

"So pretty." She softly moaned, before placing all of it into her mouth. The two were so entangled into each other spider web of passion that they never noticed Tess standing in the restroom watching through the foggy shower glass doors. Tess head went back and forth as if she had BoBo's private in her mouth, stroking it like Angie. Tess skirt was short enough that she could tease her own kitty, which made it good for her due to the fact that she never wore panties.

Tess sat on the edge of the toilet and inserted her middle finger in her moistness, and licked her tongue out while watching the two.

Angie cupped BoBo's two small friends in her mouth while allowing her tongue to graze his shaft.

"Oh shit, oooohh..." Weak at the knees, BoBo moaned, as he pulled her up by her braids, spinning her around mashing her face against the shower glass. Quickly BoBo went down on his knees as the water fell on his face which made the sensation more enjoyable for the both of them.

BoBo spread Angie's legs apart and gently French-kissed her wetness. Loud moans filled the small bathroom.

"Bo...Bo...Bo...Bo..." Angie panting as her chest heaved up and down. Her body shivered uncontrollably. BoBo came up and inserted his throbbing penis into her hot, steamy love box. Angie screamed out loudly.

"Woo...wait! Too much." but BoBo ignored her request. He was caught in the heat of the moment.

Tess was about to reach her climax, she took her finger out of her dripping wet hot box, and softly moaned, "BoBo," Tess inserted it back in to her hot oven, then pulled it out again and placed her finger in her mouth smiling now calling, Angie's name.

"That's it baby, get it!" Angie cried out in passion.

Tess was about to explode, cum was coming down her leg like water from a faucet. Her body trembled out of control , as her head went back and knocked the small vast that was stationed on the back of the toilet onto the floor, causing a crashing noise to disturb Angie's and BoBo's love fight in the shower. Quickly she gathered herself, and ran out of the house. Angie opened her eyes only to see a broken vase.

"Tess...Tess!" She screamed, as she was force to step out of the shower, bringing their sexcapade to an early end.

CHAPTER 4 All About Da Money

"Quality Production, Tori speaking. How may I help you?" Tori the receptionist asked with an inviting tone.

"Yes, uumm...my name is, Cassel Brown. I'm with, 'Over the Top Films' and I'm trying to contact Travis Hayes concerning his company directing a movie." Cassel explained.

"Hold please. I'm transferring you now."

Cassel listened to elevator music while being placed on hold. This would be his first time actually speaking with Mr. Hayes, since he first saw him at the premier of, 'Wrong Side of the Lake'. He continued to listen until he heard a click.

"Travis Hayes, how may I help you?"

"Mr. Hayes, this is, Cassel Brown, with 'Over the top Films'. We met a year ago at your premier of Wrong Side of the Lake, and I enjoyed the directing part of that film so much that I would like for you to direct my new movie." There was a long pause. Travis was trying to put a face with the name. Then he snapped his finger, reaching into his top right drawer retrieving a small iron box of business cards, thumbing through them until finding Mr. Brown's card.

"Yes, Mr. Brown, how are you doing?"

"I'm fine thanks for asking."

"May I ask you what the film is about? And, when is the production? And," Travis paused, thinking of how to say what he needed to say without offending Mr. Brown, "First let me say this. I don't do Urban Hood movies." Travis strongly stated. He was doing everything in his power to forget about his treacherous life style he once lived. All the murders, drug selling, and turning out young women, was something he wanted no parts of. Travis even thought back to all the time he spent in prison, state and federal. He did two years in the state, got out did an additional three in the state, then finally the big boys got him. The FEDS. He served eight and a half years with them. If not for his brother Big O, he would have gotten life.

Travis, AKA King, was a three time convicted felon. He vowed to stay clear of all danger. He refused to relive that life even in a movie. Although, he made millions with his two companies, it was something about that life that he loved so much. The rush of the streets.

"I do understand. However, this movie is about a woman who finds love, gets married, only to find out that her husband is a woman who has had a sex change at the early age of eighteen."

King Laughed, "Send me the script."

"What's your email address?"

"Aqualityking@yahoo.com."

"I'm sending it now. What will be your price if you decide to direct this movie?"

"For me to be on location for three months or more, it will cost you $400,000. That's a $150,000 out of the four up front, an additional fifty upon arrival, and the other two when production is completed." Travis insisted. His price was non-negotiable.

"I'll email you the contract also. Hope to hear from you within the next couple days."

At that moment King turned to his lap top, typed in his password to retrieve his emails, and pulled up the script. He leaned back in his extra large soft leather chair and begun to read the script, until Tori buzzed his office.

"Mr. Hayes," seductively she called out his name. He knew she was in-love with him; however, he never mixed sex in the work place. "I'm preparing to leave for the evening. Will there be anything else before I go? I mean anything?"

King smiled, as he continued to look at the script. "No thank you. Have a great weekend." he insisted.

As Tori was clicking the speaker off, he managed to hear her say," It would be better, if you would come home with me, and give me some of that dick." Again he smiled at the same time buzzing her back. "I heard that." Tori never responded; she rushed out of the office.

King decided that the script was good enough for him to direct.

He got up, packed his belonging, and headed for the door. He wanted to know who the actors and actresses, were going to be. Also he felt that the role of Sandy, the woman who found out her husband was a man needed to be played by, Tarija P. Henson. Therefore, he decided to head for Atlanta tonight. He had to call Cassel back to see what his budget was, but waited to contact him.

King left work and drove to his apartment, which was close to his office on Elvis Presley Blvd, instead of going to his mansion in South Wynn, a gated community on Hacks Cross. He never spent too many nights there due to his past life. King was always leery of being followed. He felt if someone caught him at the mansion they would have hit the mother load, and he couldn't allow them to live behind that one.

By his home being in a gated community, that had a guard at the gate who had to call you before allowing someone to come on the premises, he still felt unsafe. King had that ghetto mentality that everyone could be bribed. Therefore he spent most of his nights at his downtown apartment, which his brother and his soon squad would stop by from time-to-time.

King exited his C1550, and walked to his apartment door only to find that it was slightly cracked. Without his 40 cal in hand, king felt that he could be walking into a trap. He turned to walk away but heard a familiar voice; a female. King also knew it would be a female that would get your noodle knocked loose, however, he peeped through the cracked door, realizing that it was Tresha, Lil Dillin's woman whom was also the female commentator from Moneeka's book signing.

King entered his apartment, "What the hell?" he asked Tresha, as she stood there talking on the phone.

"Hey, King. Lil Dillin, and ya' brother went to go get something to drink and eat. They'll be right back." King rushed into his room, went into his closet and loaded his 40 cal. He didn't trust no woman. Tresha walked to his bed room and stood there looking sexy.

"Who left my damn door open?" he asked. Tresha just shrugged her shoulders.

"Lil Dillin, might have when he walked out." King began packing his clothes for his trip. Tresha stood there on the phone. "King," Tresha said seductively, while tugging on her booty shorts and pulling her wife beater down, "Uumm, do you have a girl friend?" she said shyly, crossing her legs, looking him up and down.

"Why?" He asked nonchalantly, not even looking her way.

"Cause my girlfriend needs a good man in her life." she paused, "and since you don't have anybody..."

"1-I'm not a good man. 2-I've never had trouble getting pussy. And 3, I don't do hood chicks anymore." he placed a fake smile on his face.

Tresha puckered her lips, rolled her eyes, and pivoted on her heels and walked off. Moments later Lil Dillin, and Big O, came busting through the front door, as King was coming out of his bedroom with his luggage.

"Where you going, Big Bruh?" Big O asked, needless to say, King ignored his question. Big O noticed the frown, "What's wrong now?"

"Outside! Both of you!" King stressed. Lil Dillin and Big O, looked at each other shaking their heads as they walked out onto the balcony. "How many times have I asked you two not to bring them damn, chicken heads over to this spot?" Lil Dillin got ready to answer the question, "Wait, to top that shit off, one of you idiots left the fucking door cracked for someone to come up in this bitch and take every fucking thing!"

King was heated.

"Why you trippin'? It ain't like we still in the game." Big O said, preparing to light a blunt. King snatched it, and threw it over the balcony.

"Ah bruh, that was some purp!"

"In the game, out the game," he paused, "never mind. You two always doing something to piss me off. I'm heading to, Atlanta."

"What time we leave." Lil Dillin said excitedly.

"Not you two, me. You two going to stay here and close that deal at FED-X. Fred Smith has already gave our company two million up front. So you two idiots are going to stay on top of our employee's until the job is finish. That's when we'll get our other six million."

"I'ma take care of it bruh." Big O said with confidence, patting King on the shoulders. Although he had no faith in either of the two, they were family. He knew those two would fuck up a wet dream. Especially Lil Dillin, his nephew.

"If your mother wasn't my oldest sister, I would have been cut your lil wild ass off!"

Lil Dillin stood there smiling with those golds in his mouth, with his hands in the air. "Unk, what? What I do now?" He could never take anything his uncle said to him serious. Lil Dillin thought that everything was a joke. He knew his uncle would always have his back. Lil Dillin father was the reason King got in the drug game. But after he got killed, "King and Big O killed the man that gunned his father down. He promised his sister that he would always take care of him, no matter what.

"Just handle the business!" King said, as he walked out the door slamming it behind him.

"Fuck, Unk! Let's get this party started!" Lil Dillin shouted, walking up on Tresha and grabbing her ass.

B'Shone

CHAPTER 5 Get'n Horny

Moneeka and Angie arrived at Hartsfield, Atlanta airport, and stood at the baggage claim looking for someone holding a sign with her name on it. To her surprise, today wasn't her lucky day. They gathered their luggage and headed for the exit. They exited the double sliding glass doors, and saw a line of Checker Taxi Cabs parked out front waiting for their next customer. The two walked to the front of the line and got into the first cab. The driver got out and placed their luggage in the trunk.

"Where to, ladies?" the super dark, tall and bald gentleman asked.

"Marriot Marquee, on Peach Tree and Lennox." Moneeka said, unfolding her arms, as she dials her agent number. No answer.

The taxi driver emerged into traffic trying to go with the follow. Angie and Moneeka sat in silence. Moneeka pondered over why her agent didn't show. This was the first time that she ever had to take a taxi away from the airport--since her first book came out. She was always used to being chauffeured, and riding in limo's, upon arriving in a different city. Moneeka was boiling hot. She had a few choice words for Linda her agent.

Angie felt the tension in the taxi, but truly didn't care. She knew that Moneeka could be a real bitch at times; however, she decided to loosen the mood. Just as the driver drove past Club Strokers, Angie laughed and pointed.

"We're going there tonight! I'ma watch me a freak show up in that bitch!" she said excitedly. "I'ma learn me some new moves so I can put'em on BoBo." She wiggled in the back seat, pretending to be a stripper making her booty pop. She noticed Moneeka slightly smiling. "Yeah girl, we can learn some new moves from them hoes, for our men...wait I mean my man, ya' conceited ass, is too good for one." she said playfully hitting her on the shoulders, "or you like bumping pussy." Angie looked her up and down. As they erupted into laughter.

"Oh, no. I love men. And I know how to drop it like it's hot." Moneeka, stiff and tight body tried to shake what her mother gave her which was a lot, but to no avail, it didn't look sexy.

"Please stop. Bitch go find your soul, then try again."

"Oh gosh, Angie. I really don't have soul in me."

"At least not a black one."

"What happen?"

"What happen is you got ya' ass on a pedestal, as if you're God's, gift to men. Scratch that, to the whole fuckin' world."

"I do not." Moneeka pouted.

"You do. You thought by dissing that fine ass chocolate nigga at the club the other night bout his car, that you were better than him."

"Did you see what he was driving?" Moneeka rolled her eyes in

32

disgust.

"See that's the shit I'm talking about. If a nigga ain't riding; a Benz or Caddy, in ya eyes he ain't shit." Angie stressed, "That's why his sexy ass walked pass you."

Angie had really put something on her mind. Moneeka sat there in silence thinking. She knew that she had acted out of character. Moneeka thought if she continued to act conceited that she would die a lonely woman. No one would actually love her for her with that jacked up attitude. All every man would want from her would be a piece of booty. Something had to change.

The taxi driver pulled into the Marriot, and drove to the valet.

"That'll be thirty five dollars." Moneeka reach and her purse and pulled out two twenties.

"Here, keep the change."

Quickly he got out of the Taxi and retrieved their luggage, placing it on the bellboy's gold and red cart. He looked Moneeka up and down in her tight Baby Phat jeans and smiled.

"I'll be more than happy to be your man." said the Taxi driver.

"Awe, no thank you." Moneeka frowned, turning her nose up.

"Have a nice day, ladies." he looked away depressed.

At that moment Moneeka's phone rang. She quickly glanced down at the caller I.D. "My agent." She told Angie, as she pressed the speaker. "Hello."

"Moneeka, I'm so sorry I forgot to have the chauffeur there to pick you up. I was out of town and running late." she explained, talking extremely fast. "I'm so glad you made it, and plus I have some great news for you." Linda the agent said, excitedly. "I got you a starring role in that new movie everybody is trying to be a part of."

Moneeka was trying to act as if she wasn't impressed. "And that is?" she asked nonchalantly.

"Fooled! And the director is the same director from 'The Wrong Side Of The Lake'"

Moneeka wanted to jump for joy, screaming however, she tried to keep her cool. She knew this was the big break she'd been waiting for.

"So what does it pay?" she asked.

"Three hundred thousand!" Linda yelled.

Angie's eyes widened.

Moneeka pressed mute, and screamed, "Yes! Now that's what I'm talking about!" excitedly she said, "I don't do cab drivers. I do directors. And I'm going to get him!"

"You may want the director but he may not want you." Angie stated, as she walked off heading to the counter to check in. Moneeka walked behind Angie rubbing her bow hips.

"Angie, please. They all want this." She discreetly flirted with a white man walking out of the hotel. "Hey, handsome."

The man stumbled over his own feet lusting after her beauty. She

34

pressed mute again. "Okay, I'm at the hotel, just drop the script off."

"I'm in route now." Linda said, as she hung up the phone. They checked in, went to their separate rooms, and unwound for the night.

***

Moneeka sat in her bed reading the script and begun to get horny, after reading the sex scene she had in the movie. "I hope the leading man is fine and hung. I might decide to spread my legs after all." Although, Moneeka hasn't been sexually active in two years, she was now ready for something new and to give love a try. She continued to read the script at the same time massaging her warmth. "Mumm," she moaned, titling her head back, dropping the script to the floor. As her silver bullet tingled her vagina. She spread her legs eagle wide and turned the bullet up on high. Within minutes, loud moans could be heard in the hallway. Moneeka was pleasing herself as if she had nine inches of hard, raw beef steak shoved up in her neatly trimmed wet: spot. "Ohhh, mumm, awe..." again she moaned out in passion. It felt so good to her that she started talking to her bullet. "Daddy, it's been so long. Get it baby! Get this! ahhh! YES! YES! YES!" She exploded and creamy thick cum shot out of her as she screamed to the top of her lungs. Her body trembled like never before. With her eyes stuck in the back of her head, her hands locked, as if to be paralyzed, with the slightest touch, she came over and over again, as she tried to release the bullet. This was an experience like none other. Moneeka hadn't used her bullet, her finger, or nothing else since her last friend- two years ago. It was as if she was a virgin; tight and rite.

B'Shone

CHAPTER 6 Da Boss

'Tyler Perry Studio's, the banner read across the top of the entrance. King drove in only to be stopped at the guard shack. The guard took his I.D., gave King a visitor's badge and pointed him in the direction of Studio 69. He drove back and recognized prop's that he once used before and some he hasn't. Although he had directed many movies before, but never in Atlanta, he was hoping to get a chance to see Tyler Perry himself.

Approaching Studio 69, in his red rented Chevy Impala; he was greeted by Cassel Brown and his assistant.

"I'm glad you made it. Get in." Cassel said, riding in a small golf cart. "I'm taking you to the back were all the actors and actresses, are going over there lines." King got and as they drove to the back where a large group of males and females stood around rehearsing for the movie. Cassel hired several extras just in case they needed more.

"Alright, I need everyone's attention." Cassel said, sitting in a black leather chair. Everyone stopped what they were doing and turned their attention toward him. "I want to thank everyone for coming out for rehearsal, and to congratulate all of you on making the cut." Applause filled the room. "However, I hope you all conduct yourselves as professionals." They all smiled and nodded. "I also want everyone to know that, Travis Hayes," he pointed to King, "Will be directing this movie for us. I'm sure everyone knows of all his movies." Again applause filled the large room.

"Thank you all so much." King humbly said, "If anyone has any questions, please feel free to ask." He paused, "Since there are no[1] question let's make this movie number one at the box office." King said as he and Cassel turned and walked off.

"So what do you think? Nice looking cast right?"

"Not bad at all." King stated, "But what is the budget? Can I get Tarija P. Henson, for the leading lady?"

"It's in the budget. But I have a rising star coming on board as the leading lady."

King placed a smirk on his face, "Where is she?"

"She had a previous engagement. But will be here later on today."

"Two things: Is she pretty? And can she act?"

"Both." Cassel smiled.

***

Moneeka walked into the small private conference room and stood at the podium and thanked everyone for coming out to her book release.

"At my last signing, I read a couple of paragraphs from chapter five, and I would like to read a couple of more for you guys if it's okay?" "Yes," the crowd screamed.

Moneeka started to reading from chapter five, "Robin's temperature was boiling hot. After she witness her husband perform the way he did with Micole, Robin knew that his love for her wasn't the same any more. Needless to say, Robin had to find out." Moneeka looked out into the audience and notice a few frowning faces. She even heard the woman on the front row.

"I would have shot the shit out of his ass!" the fat lady in the front row shouted. Moneeka eyes widened in shock. She felt good knowing she had captured her audience's attention so quickly. They were very much in tune with her reading. Angie stood back off to the side surprised and amazed at their reaction.

Moneeka continued, "Robin, gathered her skirt and removed herself from her home. She drove around crying for an hour until turning into 'Candy Coated' sex store, by Candy Burris. She rushed in and got herself a few new sex toys. That's when she glanced to the left of her and noticed a Super woman thong and bra set—the same kind that was on her floor when her husband Shone had Micole's ass in the air. Robin realized that it came out of there.

"Give me that," she pointed, "in a medium, now!"She angrily told the clerk. She purchased it and left the store. Robin called Shone's cell phone to let him know that she was on her way home; giving him the heads up."

Again she was interrupted by the lady on the front row. "I wouldn't have called his sorry black ass! I would have been calling the muthafuckin' morgue! Cause he would have been one dead ass niggah!"

"I'm glad to see someone paying attention." Moneeka joked, as the audience erupted in laughter. Moneeka continued reading.

"Robin walked threw her living room door, to the sound of Sexual Healing, by Marvin Gaye blasting."

"Hey baby," Shone, said to her as he stepped into the shower, dancing to the tune. "How was your day?"He asked. Robin pretended to act as if she cared to converse with him.

"It was surprising." Robin said as she quickly got out of her clothes and put on her Super Woman outfit and high heels. She tossed her clothes over by the lounge chair where she noticed her thongs from earlier. Anger came rushing back over her at once, however she kept her cool. She got in her bed and laid on her side with her head resting in her right hand.

"If Shone don't fuck me better than he fucked, that bitch!" She stopped and shook that image out of her head. It hurt her heart to see the way he made love to Micole. Robin knew that he never made love to her that good. She knew because she was turned on by his moves.

Shone walked into their bedroom, and notice his wife laying across their bed looking as sexy as she could, with her legs spread wide open.

"On your knees now!" Robin demanded.

"Baby, what's gotten in you?" Shone said smiling.

"On your knees now!" Robin repeated, patting her hot pocket.

Shone was baffled. He reached for his t-shirt that was lying next to Robin, but she quickly tucked it between her legs."I want my pussy ate now! On your knees!" She pondered for a quick second if Micole had this much trouble getting him to taste all her juices that poured out of her pink oven.

Slowly Shone got down on all fours as Robin laid back once again spreading her legs as wide as they could go. Shone gently started tasting her Black Berry Cobbler, "muummm," Robin moaned. "Faster!" she insisted, but Shone glanced up at her, she took both of her legs and wrapped them around his neck and began choking him. Robin had her I-phone in hand playing the sex movie that him and Micole had produced earlier. Shone wrestled to get free. But Robin had a death grip on his neck.

"Baby wait!" Shone choked.

"Eat it like you eat that bitch pussy!" Robin yelled. "Eat it damn it!" Robin eyes were blood shot red, and filled with tears, as she let his neck go. "I've given your sorry ass every fabric of me. And this is how you repay me?" Robin cried, as she stood over her husband body looking down at him squirming on the floor. A few more seconds he would have been dead. "

The fat lady on the front row once again yelled out, "She should have killed his bitch ass! I'd choked his ass until he couldn't breathe!" The audience erupted again in laughter- that is most of the women.

Moneeka placed a devilish smirk on her face, as she continued to stare out into the audience.

"I will stop here for now. Again I would like to thank you all for your support." She smiled, as she continued to listen to the angry woman on the front row.

"Damn! That's it?"

"For now. You will have to finish reading the book to find out what happen at the end." She winked at the crowd. "Also, be on the lookout for my new movie, FOOLED, coming out this thanksgiving. Again thank you all for coming out. I love you." Moneeka sashayed away from the podium as howls and cheers of applause filled the room.

"Girl you shocked the shit outta me. You did a great job." Angie said. "I'm impressed. But that lady on the front row was pissed at you."

"I always get that kind of reaction." Moneeka bragged.

Angie rolled her eyes, shaking her head at the same time, "You never seem to amaze me with that nasty mouth of yours. One day someone is gonna break ya' siddity ass down." Angie said walking away from her. She hated Moneeka way of thinking.

"What I say? I only told the truth." Moneeka said, walking behind Angie.

CHAPTER 7 Da Plug

"Say, Thunder Cat, I'm heading to Cashville to holla at one of my old chicks for a couple of hours." Big O told Lil Dillin, "I'll holla back at 'cha when I'm on my way back. And if my brother calls, don't tell him where I'm at. Just say I'm knee deep in some ass, and yes we took care of the business."

"I got'cha," Lil Dillin told him hanging up the phone.

At that moment Big O hopped on 1-4O heading to Nashville to meet ex-wifey. Reca Gant. Reca was Big O's heart. That is until he got sentenced to 15 years in the FEDS. With that bitterness sat in his heart for her. However, Reca cared deeply for him; she hated the fact that he placed his brother King before her. Reca felt that King was the reason for Big O going to federal prison. She never got over the fact that he accepted the leadership role instead of King. She hated him because King got 10 years and Big O got 15 years. Big O knew his brother was a three time convicted felon. And if he took the leadership role, he would have been doing life in prison. Big O wasn't having that. And for that reason she left him in the mist of his storm. PRISON.

Two and a half hours later, Big O pulled up on the corner of Galatim Road and Sharp Avenue; where he saw his main man, Toledo Swerv standing outside of the old BBQ pit. Swerv walked around to the passenger side of Big O's cream Range Rover and hopped in.

"Big...Bi...Big O." Swerv stuttered, "What's gu...gu...gud?"

"Same ole shit. Money. What's been up wit 'cha?" Big O asked, rolling and blunt.

"Mane, I'm gu...gud. I see ya' ride."

Big O, Range Rover was sitting pretty on some chrome 22's, peanut butter guts, four 15's in the trunk. Beating 8 Ball and MJG, Lay it Down. Big O lit the blunt, took a couple of pulls then passed it to Swerv. Swerv took a long hard pull, coughed and started talking like a normal man.

"This is some real good shit!" He said loudly.

"Is anybody at 701 right now?" Big O asked.

"Naw. Erra-body at the Under Ground. You know, Lil...Lil... Paul is throwing at party down there?"

"Naw, I didn't know, but let me holla back at 'cha lata. I got something to handle." Big O said given Swerv dap. "Keep it my nigga." Swerv jumped out and walked back into the pit.

Moments later Big O turned on to 12th Avenue South, and Edge Hill to see ex-wifey. As he got ready to get out of his Rover he cocked the hammer back on his 45. He checked his rear view mirror, looking for any unexpected trouble. He hasn't been in Nashville in the last 13 years, but he was sure he still had a few haters that wanted him out the way. He quickly hopped out looking over his shoulder as he made it to

Reca's door. He rang the door bell.

"Coming!" Reca yelled out as she rushed to the door. "Who is it?"

"Big O." he said, with a deep tone. Reca quickly opened the door with an unexpected look on her face. She thought she would never see him again the way she turned her back on him. Needless to say, today was her lucky day. She stood there gazing at him without saying a word. All the hatred she harbored for him vanished at the sound of his name."May I come in." again his deep voice made her buckled at the knees.

Big O stood 6'2, 310 pounds, long braids with his 'I know I got money swag.

"Sur...sure come on in." Before he had a chance to take one step into her home she jumped into his arms pleading her cause. "O, I'm sorry!" she cried, " I know that I was suppose to ride or die with Big O," Tears rolled down her face, but Big O never said a word. "Please say something! Don't hate me. I sent you some money, and cards letting you know that I was thinkin' of you! Please!" Still he remained quiet.

He came for one thing. Sex. And once he got it, he was going to bounce.

Reca had some of the best loving Big O had ever had, that's why he drove 200 miles for some sex. She would do any and everything for him sexually. And tonight he was going to try to relive those moments; however, he knew that he didn't have much time.

Being that Reca was only 5'5, Big O handled her as if she was lite-weight. He walked with her still in his arms to her bedroom, and threw her down on her bed. Her peanut butter skin, wide hips, big ass, and short hair instantly turned him on. Big O took off his Polo sweat shirt, and Reca knew exactly what time it was. She felt if he would come this far for some sex she might have a chance at getting him back. She commence to working her way out of her too small Daises Dukes. Panties, she never wore. Reca never bothered to take her halter top off, she just started right in on his Polo sweat pants, pulling them down to his knees. She wasted no time sipping on his long, fat, black straw. She was trying her best to make the milk come gushing out of it.

Memories came rushing back over her all at once. Reca was gulping his entire penis causing him to back away. "Ahh." Big O moaned.

The sensation and tingling feeling he had just received made him ready to bang her back out. "Damn girl. Turn around." He insisted.

Seductively she smiled and said, "Anyway you want it, it's yours." With haste she turned around and reached back with her right hand and spread her butt cheeks apart for him. Big O inserted himself in her hot box only to hear her yelp out in pain. "Please go slow. It's been a while." She cried out. A look appeared on his face as to say 'Bitch stop lyin'. That's when he went all in. He slammed in and out of her as if he was punishing her for old and new. The rippled in her cheeks looked like baby tidal waves, everything he slammed into her, which turned him on even more.

"Yes!" Big O screamed out. The two had been going for an good twenty minutes before Reca started begging him to slow down.

"O, please, wait.. ahh..O, slow... please...ahhh!" she shouted, "Too much!" It was too late. Big O pulled out and released semen on her back as she fell forward and he collapsed on her bed.

Big O mumbled to himself, "Awe, she was worth the drive." he said glancing up at the ceiling. Reca got up and walked into the bathroom to clean herself. Moments later she walked out with a clean, warm towel and wiped his penis off. But when she came back into the room she found him putting on his clothes.

"O, please don't tell me ya' gettin' ready to go?"Reca said, as she sat on the edge of the bed cleaning his beef steak. He reached into his pocket and passed her some weed.

"Here roll this up." Reca walked into the living room, sat on the couch and reached under the seat and pulled out a Nike shoe box top and started rolling them a blunt. Big O's phone rang. He noticed the number and smiled.

"Big O, are you back to stay?" Reca asked, letting her tongue glide across the top of the blunt as she stuck it together.

"Perfectly rolled." He took the blunt. "Hello," he coughed as he answered his I-Phone. "Okay I'm over someone house right now."He stood placing the blunt in her ashtray. Reca picked it up, "but I know where you're at." Big O said, looking at Reca laying back on the cough massaging her hot spot.

"We're not finish, O." She whispered.

"Okay." Big O said, hanging up the phone. "Girl, you still the same." he smiled at her. He stood in his same spot fumbling in his pockets as to be looking for something. Then his eyes scanned her room before he snapped his fingers. "Damn, I left it in the truck. Hand me my 45."

"Why? What's wrong?" Reca looked concerned.

"Ah nothing. I left something in my truck, but I'm not going out there without that." Reca gave him his 45, with a smile. He cracked her door, peeped out, then looked back at her. "I'll be right back."

Big O hit the remote start and jumped into his Rover, reach over the sun visor, got another blunt that he had rolled lit and backed out.

Reca rushed to the door screaming, "O, please don't gooooo!" She stood in the door naked, from their sex fight.

A 15-year-old boy from across the hall came outside to see what all the commotion was about. To his surprise, he saw Reca's nude body. Lustfully, he stared on.

Reca notice his erection through his gym-shorts. "What the hell you looking at?" She walked in the house and slammed the door.

Twenty minutes later, Big O pulled up on Lishey Avenue and Settles Court; the Sam Levy Homes, aka, SC Projects. He turned into the drive making a right heading to the back circle but pulled over in front of the Dollar General store. There, is where he saw Nekka Battles, a brown skin, 5'9" stallion. Nekka was thick as any woman her height could be. There wasn't a word in the dictionary that could describe her thickness. Her short bob hair style displayed her high cheek bones, which accented her beautiful smile.

Nekka was a known hustler. She hustled better than your average dealer. She even had her own crew which consisted of all females. And they weren't afraid to go to war with any woman, or man.

Big O let his window down and called out to her, "Nekka, what it do?" Due to the darkness she squinted her eyes trying to get a visual on whom it was calling her name. She didn't recognize the Rover. Slowly, she reached for her 40 Glock.

"Who that?" she screamed.

"Big O."

"Big O. Awe that's my dawg!" Nekka rushed over to the truck." Boy, ya ass almost got it," she said while hopping up in his Rover. "How long you been out? I heard you and ya' brother was doing big thang in Memphis."

"We good. I've been beating the streets for ten mouths now."

"What you doing in Nashville?" Nekka asked and Big O smiled.

"Come on, Nek, you know your boy."

Nekka gave him a crazy look, "A'ight, O, be careful. Shit ain't the same as it was when you were running back and forth from Memphis, to Nashville." Nekka tried to give her long time friend some sound advice as she hopped out of his rover.

"I got'cha." Big O said, still smoking his blunt."

Nekka stood outside of his truck and signaled for one of her workers to come over. Tiffany, her cousin came over with haste. "Give

49

me that money, you got on you." Nekka told her. "Big O, I know you don't need this, but put this in ya' pocket." she tossed him a wad of money. "I can't let you leave without giving you something. It's 3500. You still my nigga although you left the hood." She joked as she turned to walk away. "Tell ya sexy brother, I said come get some of this pussy."

Big O smiled, as she walked away mumbling to herself, "I'll get that pussy for him."

Big O then pulled around to the circle and found Lil Paul standing next to his brand new Super Man Benz that he bought from Shaq himself.

A group of young goons were posted at his side, alone with several hood rats trying to see who Lil Paul is taking to in the crib .

Big O got out and walked over to him. They showed one another love as Paul walked Big O back over to his truck. "Come on. I'ma ride with you. Drive off."

"What about ya' car?"

"Nigga, you know my shit safe in the projects."

Big O reached into his ashtray, but quickly forgot that his partner didn't smoke. He respected him too much to light it up now.

"Ride ova' by Top Dawg on Buchanan. I need to check on something."

Big O agreed and the conversation began. "So ya' through with the street life?" Lil Paul asked.

"It depends." Big O responded.

"On what, Big Man?"

"What it is? And how much?"

Lil Paul nodded. He always loved Big O's hustle. Big O was the one person he could trust if shit hit the fan."What if I tell you I got that, Dog Food, china white, uncut; raw. That will at least take a seven.

And you can get it for," he paused, "85 a pop." Big O had a slight smirk on his face. "That is, if you plan on beating them streets again."

"How many you gonna throw my way?" Big O asked, letting the sunroof back so the fresh breeze could come in.

"Nut'n less than forty at a time. That's the only way."

Quickly Big O asked, "Can you get them to Memphis?"

"You know it."

"Make it happen." Again they dapped it up.

"What about ya' brother? I don't need him breathing down my neck."

"Don't worry 'bout him. We still run the 1300 block of Hyde Park."

Moments later they pulled in front of Top Dawg and quickly left.

Lil Paul had seen some trouble that he didn't need right now. He refused to allow his man to go back to the FEDS over some bullshit. The McQuiddy Boys were his rivals. There were about twenty of them standing in front of the club. They had beef with Lil Paul over the Preston Taylor,

JC Napier and University Courts. The projects they wanted but couldn't take away from Lil Paul. His money was too long and his hit men were always on point. Just not tonight. If they could catch him slipping like this it would have made their night.

"I got some small beef with the McQuiddy Boys right now. So I want you to stay clear of them whenever you're in town. If they get the news that you're down with me again, they wouldn't hesitate to take you out."

Big O drove to Wade's Market at the corner of 12th Avenue North and Buchanan. He pulled into the market and turned the engine off.

"Come on. We got to cross the street to, Cyn's Soul Food," Lil Paul smiled, then winked at Big O, "this is my joint too. Plus I want you to see the work."

Two hours later Big O was on 1-40 West heading back to Memphis. He called Lil Dillin. "It's on. Go get the 1300 block house ready. I'm on my way back. Nigga, it's on. I fell in love with a 40-year-old virgin and she looked like a China White Doll." Big O smiled. As he hung up, his phone rang, "Hello." He placed it on speaker.

"If you think you gonna fuck me and leave like that you got me fucked up. I'll get you back!" Reca cried on the phone.

"You already did when you dipping on me while I was in prison! Bitch!"

B'Shone

CHAPTER 8 It's War

Malcolm stood posted outside of his trap house on the 1300 block of Hyde Park watching his foot soldiers maneuvering through traffic, as people collected money and sold narcotics. Kelly P, Malcolm's look out man stood at the corner of Hyde Park and Chelsa looking for the laws, and any unexpected or unwanted trouble.

"Ah...ah... Malcolm," Kelly P stuttered, as he spoke threw his walkie talkie, "A cream Range Ro..Rover, and Caddy ju..just turned on the street."

Quickly Malcolm threw his hands up signaling for everybody to be on the lookout for any trouble. Some of his soldiers rushed to get their choppers, while the others hustled to put the dope away. Malcolm stepped into his safe house. The Rover and the all black Caddy pulled to the end of the block and parked in a half boarded up white and brick house.

Kelly P made it to the safe house where Malcolm was posted.

"Ah ain't tha...tha...that's, Kings, old house?"

Malcolm nodded, "Yep, but that's not, King." he said staring out the living room window at the two men getting out the backseat of the Rover. They immediately began unboarding the rest of the house.

"They must have sold that joint. Hell it's been like that for a minute. Damn I should've bought it." Malcolm stated, before taking a closer look. That's when he saw Lil Dillin hoping out of his Caddy tucking his 4O cal under his shirt. Being that Lil Dillin only stood 5'7, and extra thin, his 4O was easily noticed. Dillin walked on the porch took a breath of fresh air, and started on his breakfast; a blunt.

Finally, Big O got out of his Range with a thick yellow, Brazilian chick who stepped out of the passenger side. Her six inch stiletto's with the gold and black straps that came all the way up her legs stopping at her knees, accented the black and gold, short body suit that wrapped around her curves nicely; flawless. She walked over to the curb and stood next to Big O, whom was on the phone looking down the street.

At that moment Foulks & Son's moving truck turned onto the street. O waved his hand for the truck to come further down.

"Daddy, after this are we going to Vegas?" asked the Brazilian chick.

He smiled, devilish, "Yeah, after you do that trick with ya tongue again. Over and over."

"I know damn well they're not moving back on the fuckin' dope track!" Malcolm said, as he continued to observe Big O's action.

"That bi...bitch sho' is fi...fine." Kelly P said, as Malcolm looked upside his head.

"Shut ya' stuttered ass up! Come on!" Malcolm told his crew. They all walked outside and stood by their cars cocking the hammer back on their pistols.

"I hope we're not ge...ge...getting ready for waaaar." Kelly P said nervously.

The truck pulled in front of King's old house and started to unload the furniture. Two couches, one table, a stove and a refrigerator.

The driver of the truck stood in the living room talking to Big O.

"Lil' Paul went on and sent you a hundred instead of forty." The driver said moving closer to the first couch. "He said if you have any problem call him at this number." He gave Big O a phone number for him to call. "No one calls this number but you, also the ticket is seventy five. Now with that being said I'm ready to go." The driver leaned over to Big O and whispered in his ear, "Is she a freak or ya' main squeeze?"

Big O looked at her and said to him, "You want some of that?" The driver nodded yes. O turned to his chick, "Say baby girl, go on and ride with him. He's leaving now heading to, Vegas. I'll be leaving next week." She was smiling from ear to ear.

"Okay daddy." she cooed.

"Take care of him like you always do me."

"Anything you say." She kissed Big O on the cheek and left with the driver. But not before the driver turned around to Big O.

"25 is in that couch, 25 in that one, 25 in the stove and 25 in the frig." The driver said as he took the Brazilian chick by the hand and escorted her to his truck.

Big O observed Malcolm and his crew walking toward their spot.

"Thunder Cat," Big O called out. Lil Dillin raced out to the porch.

"What it is? Who want some trouble?!" He looked and seen Malcolm coming and upped his 40 cal. "Gud, I been looking for some trouble all day."

As Malcolm approached the two, he seen the 40. He knew that they were ready for whatever came their way. Trouble was something they loved.

Slowly Malcom raised his hands, "Woo... I came in peace, Big O."

Malcolm said with his hands held high smiling. He wasn't afraid of trouble he was just the kind of person to play his cards right. "So y'all back in the game?" Big O nodded, yes. "But I thought ya' brother said this block was mines?" Malcolm looked confused. He knew Big O went against his brother on everything when it came to the streets, he just wanted to know if they were about to get it on. That's when he observed a few more of Big O's goons pulling up hopping out of an all black van.

"Well my brother said that the block was big enuff for all of us to make some money." Big O paused for effect, but got none. "So with that being said the block is still yours. We don't want none of ya' cutomers or none of your beef with, St. Louis Black." Big O smiled as Malcom's eyes widened. "What you thought I didn't know about the beef you have with the real Jack 'St Louis Black' William Jr.?" Big O stressed. "So here it is. Everything over here is yours. My customers are heavy weight dealers. They will come straight here and leave. All I'ma tell you is, don't fuck with my people, or try to serve them, because you can't. You don't have what I got." Malcolm nodded, but frowned at the same damn time.

"What you mean I can't?" Malcolm asked.

"1, they're my customers and 2, I got that raw, uncut girl, that dog food. And 3, I will cut ya' fuckin' head off if you try to stop my flow."

Big O said walking up in Malcolm's face, "if you want you can buy from me too." He then turned and walked away. Lil Dillin stood there bouncing side to side as if he was getting ready to box.

"Thunder Cat, come on. It ain't no beef..." Big O paused and smiled, "Yet." He looked at Malcolm and said, "Get at me, Mal. Let's get this money."

Malcolm turned and said to his soldiers, "We gonna see how things pan out. But I'ma get at that fat ass nigga." He wasn't happy about his new situation. Drama was brewing just down the block. Somehow he had to eliminate it before it got started.

"Wha...wha...what we gon' do?" Kelly P asked, trembling.

"First I'ma get ya' stuttering ass off the corner before we get killed or caught, then I'ma handle them!" Malcolm said, "But for now, we just gonna play it by ear." Malcolm was heated. "If I'll go to war with his Big Brother, I will definitely go to war with his ass! Everybody to the safe house."

Big O stood in the window as Malcolm and his crew congregated in the middle of the street before walking off. Lil Dillin walked up behind him with ten Kilo's in a duffle bag. He too glanced out of the window.

"What's up, Big Cuz?" Lil Dillin asked. For once he was serious. He knew he had to stay on his p's and q's.

"Shit. Just watching them clowns. They don't want it. I just hope my brother don't find out." Big O calmly stated. He never wanted to let his big brother down. Big O was the reason behind them getting caught up.

If only he would have listened, they wouldn't have gone to prison. "I just hate when me and him ain't on the same page."

"Man, Unk be trippin' but that nigga love us to death."

"This I know." Something was on Big O's mind, but Lil Dillin didn't see it.

"Go across the bridge to West Memphis Arkansas on 18th. Get the Robinson Boyz for me. Tell Tony that I said to send his hit squad, and to call me."

"What you got brewing?" Curiosity was eating at Dillin.

"We're gonna lay low for a few days. I want Tony's crew to just hang out over here in the trap. Not to sell dope, just to hang." Big O said.

"Well I'ma take these ten with me. Lucus want to buy these ten now.

So I'm heading to Forest City." Lil Dillin said. "I'll stop in West Memphis on my way back."

"Take one of them with you!" Big O suggested pointing to one of his goons.

B'Shone

CHAPTER 9 On Da Set

"Mo, can you please bring ya' ass on!" Angie yelled standing on the outside of Moneeka's hotel room door. She continued to beat on the door until Moneeka snatched it open frowning. She stood there in her red lace bathrobe, which revealed her matching thong and bra.

"Oh my gosh, Angie." Moneeka said, turning around and walking back into her room.

"Damn, bitch! You going to a movie shoot, not rip the fuckin' runway." Moneeka rolled her eyes as she went into the bathroom, and finish applying her ruby red lip gloss.

"Angie," she said like an annoying white girl, "I just got a call from my girl Mickey, who is a production manger of the same movie, and she told me that the director is fine as hell." Moneeka smiled, "And let's not forget rich." She rubbed her fingers together signaling money. After she finish tracing her lips with a black liner, she puckered them up,"Muum..ah nice and shiny."

"You better get me a small role in this movie." Angie stated, as Moneeka walked over to her bed and squeezed her ass in a pair of Versace pants, and a short waist t-shirt. She turned around and looked at her backside in a full length mirror, admiring the view. "Perfect. I'm sure he'll be eatin' some booty tonight." Moneeka said, rubbing her firm round butt.

Angie quickly said, "Or you'll be sucking his dick once. Because even I know that you ain't had no dick in forever, so stop all the lying." Moneeka was shocked to know that Angie knew her business so well. She had tried to camouflage her sex life from everyone by writing those freaky novels. And it worked with most people; however, Angie knew her better than she knew herself. Angie knew the only man Moneeka had slept with was Snake. Snake had popped her cherry, and made her feel loved, that is until she found him in the bed with one of her old college friends. When Moneeka burst into Snake's room looked back at her and simply said,

"Get in the bed." She was so in love with him that she thought that he was the way to make him happy. Unbeknownst to her, she left the door cracked and another one of her friends seen it, and craved for her every since.

"You don't know me like that!" Moneeka snapped. "I just don't tell you everything." She walked to the door. "Come on, girl."

Angie shook her head in disbelief, "Ya' day com...ing."

"Please don't start that again. By the way, I don't suck dick. That's gross." she paused, and thought about the last time she was with Snake and he tried to make her do that to him. Chills came over her body.

'I did learn, but didn't like it.' she thought to herself. "Unless I'm in-love and married, these lips touch nobody D.I.C.K." They were preparing to walk out the door before Angie said to her.

"I guess that did it. Cause with ya' attitude you want be married or suckin' a fat dick."

***

"This don't look good for your unknown leading lady." King said, to Cassel. It was now day one of the shoot and production had been rolling but no Moneeka. Cassel whips out his cell phone and called Linda, the agent, but got no answer. At that same moment Moneeka and Angie came strolling in like two divas. Angrily, Cassel pulled Moneeka to the side and tore into her ass.

"I don't know who in the hell you think are you! But the next time you bring your book writing ass on my set late, I'm going to send ya' back to the freaky closet that you came out of!" Angie was just an ear shot away, and heard everything. She was enjoying every bit of it. Everything Angie had ever told her was now unraveling right before her eyes.

Someone had finally stood their ground and put her in her place and disregarded her beauty. "Do we have an understanding? Because I will make it so fuckin' hard for you to get work in this industry that you'll write a book about me!"

Moneeka looked as if she wanted to cry. Every since she made that change she never had a man talk to her the way Cassel had done. Most men would over look her wrong, just to try and get some ass, but not today.

"Yes I understand, but..." she tried to explain, "I was only thirty minutes late, and I got stuck in that crazy as traffic on, Peach Tree."

"Thirty minutes early is late in filming. Get it together!" He grimaced through his teeth, "Now come on here so I can introduce you to the director who is on standby to contact Taraji P. Henson. By the way is his ex-girlfriend." Cassel lied. He looked at Angie, "Can you act?"

"Yes!" she said excitedly.

"Good, cause I might need a new leading lady."

King stood off to the side talking with some of the actors he'd worked with in the past, with his back to Cassel, whom was quickly approaching.

King looked down at his watch, then turned around. That's when their eyes met. Cassel tried to introduce the two, but it landed on deaf ear.

Neither one of them heard a word he was saying, until Angie blurred out.

"BAM! There he go!" hitting Moneeka on the back.

"Oh my gosh." Moneeka said to herself. "Please don't tell me he's the leading man?"

"Naw, bitch. You heard the man. That's the director." Angie held her stomach laughing, "Pucker up. We know who will be getting their dick sucked, and who want be getting their ass ate." Angie wouldn't stop with the insults. King stood there admiring her beauty. A smile appeared on Cassel's face. He knew he had made the right decision by the way the two gawked at each other.

Moneeka was speechless. She now knew that she had put her foot in her mouth this time. She was always told never to judge a book by its cover. And that's what she had done her entire life, now it had back fired on her. Angie continued with her smart comments.

"Get ready shiny lips and finger tips. It's gonna take a lot of dick sucking to keep this job."

"Hello, I'm King, the director." After he gently touched her soft hands, he looked down at his watch again. "Okay your trailer is over there next to mines, so go ahead and change. We're starting with your love scene next. So make sure you're on time, at all times." King told her as he turned and walked off.

"Damn, he did it again!" Angie was tickled pink. "He didn't even give you time to say shit! I told you your day was coming. And it's here!"

Moneeka was furious. She was always used to a man wanting her in the worse way, but to be turned down by the same man over and over again was eating at her like a bad plague. She knew she had to make thing right.

She walked into her trailer and headed straight for the back, where she closed the door, and cried. She had finally realized that her past life had gotten the best of her. She had lived in a superficial world.

Moneeka thought to her college days when she couldn't get a man to date her never the less, talk to her. And the attention she did receive was from guys she had absolutely no interested in.

She attended a college party were her and the rest of her unattractive girlfriends went to hang with the not so popular guys.

She had gotten so drunk that she allowed herself to be taken advantage of by another female, and was enjoying it. She knew of the female but not her name. What difference did it matter she never really knew what was happening until, the soft, wetness of the girl tongue slid in and out of her vagina, up and down her clitoris, causing her to shiver.

"Muummm..." Moneeka squirmed, "Don't stop..." Softly she moaned with her eyes closed as she was cumming. Her body exploded in pure pleasure as she squeezed the girl shoulders. Tasting all of her, the un-named female glanced up at Moneeka's face and gently said to her.

"I'll always want you." as she got up and walked out.

Moneeka came to her senses and had no clue why her panties were on the floor next to her shoes. However, she fixed her skirt got her panties and staggered to her dorm room.

'What happen to me? Did I get raped by some man?' she thought to herself, as she collapsed on her small bed. There she began her journey of writing sex novels.

Upon publishing her first novel she quickly became a bestseller of the freakiest tales. Moneeka took her first royalty check and changed her appearance. She yearned to have that attention once again, but this time, from the opposite sex. She went under the knife and got breast implants, butt injection, skin lightening, removal of her bad acne, a lace-front wig, and hazel contacts which it all made her appear to be a totally different person all together.

BOOM, BOOM, BOOM, "Let's go! You're scene is waiting!" Cassel yelled out beating on her trailer door.

Quickly she snapped back to reality, "Coming!" she yelled.

B'Shone

CHAPTER 10 Everybody Wants Her

Music buzzed through the surround sound at Montrel's Barber Shop speaker as the door chimed indicating that someone had just entered.

As usual, every male in there turned their head towards the door.

"Dammmmnnn, slim fine." One of the barbers said, as this 5'4" butterscotch, 36-26-40, pretty in the face, petite in the waist, female walked through the door. Every step she took in her red bottom stilettos made her ass look as if it was forced to wiggle in those fitting to perfection 'House of Darion jeans'. Her small perky breasts were like two peaches ready to be squeeze to see if any juice would drip out.

She stopped at chair number 5 and stared at the man getting his hair cut. Upon him opening his eyes he saw the short beauty standing in front of him. Her tongue glided around her lips slowly, as ever man in there lusted after her.

She spoke softly. "We need to talk." Her tone captured every listening man's attention. Even a few beauticians gave her low complements.

"That bitch rocking the hell outta them red bottoms. You go girl."

The man finished getting his hair cut then stood and escorted the beauty outside. They stood by his Lexus as he brushed the hair off of his shoulders.

The sexy lady stared at him. "I've never known a man with dread to stay in a barber shop as much as you do."

"Is that why you came in there putting on a show?" He said with his proper accent.

"Why didn't you tell me you were fuckin' her?"

"Check game baby girl. You and I met at a club, got drunk and high, we fucked and that was it." he paused as an older lady and her son walked pasted them. "We weren't, we ain't, and we still not in a damn relationship." he stressed to her. "Now if you just want some dick," he said grabbing his penis, "I'll be more than happy to put it up in your life. Of course, it's not free."

She gave him an evil smirk, eyed his right hand on his penis then reached in to grab it. "Believe me. if I want you, I can have you, and this." She said seductively as she squeezed his penis.

"Look, you know who I fuck with, so it is what it is." he said.

"I just want you to know, you owe me for keeping my mouth shut. I could have ended your ... whatever you two have, because it's not what you think it is." She knew how he felt about his girl, and that he would do any and everything to make her happy, and to make sure she never found out about the two of them and their sexing. She walked off, as he stood there looking at her ass.

He called out to her, "Tess," she turned around, "Can I get this dick sucked to night?"

"Fuck you, BoBo!" She yelled back. "But you can eat this hot pussy!"

BoBo knew that he fucked up badly by allowing Tess to see him and Angie having sex, knowing he slept with her too. But how could he know that the two were friends. BoBo knew that if his secret got out it would crush Angie. But how could he resist a great piece of ass. Tess truly had turned BoBo out with all the freaky things she done to him. He wanted more. BoBo knew he had to keep her quiet.

However, Tess knew more about BoBo than he suspected. She was aware of his dealing with St. Louis Black, a known drug lord and killer. Tess had been planning this move for some years now. She had been conjuring up taking a certain person out for awhile, and now had her pawn that would be used for her to get to the King, or maybe the Queen.

B'Shone

CHAPTER 11 Da Punishment

"Annnd action!" King yelled. Slowly Moneeka, who is playing the role of Janet, walked into the bedroom wearing a pair of blue and white boy shorts and a sports bra, stoping in front of her husband Stevie. He watched her as she danced for him, admiring her body.

"Get in the bed." Stevie demands. Slowly she crawls to him kissing him all over his body. Janet tried to pull his boxers off but he stops her and gets up to turn the lights off. The room was pitch-black.

"Stevie, can we make love with the lights on for once?" Janet asked.

"Tonight is our wedding night. I'm going to take good care of you." Stevie said as he laid her back on the bed, commencing to sucking on her neck. Again she tried to pull his boxers down. Once again he stops her. "I'm in control tonight baby. We don't have to rush."

"Stevie, I just want to see how pretty it is. I've never seen it only felt it." Janet said, kissing his ear lobes.

"Don't spoil the moment," he said putting his head under the cover. Seconds later Janet's shorts came off and her head instantly went back as her eyes closed. The motion of his head going up and down under the cover and Janet gripping the sheets signaled her pleasure.

"And cut!" King yelled out. Moneeka got out of the bed and was about to walk off the set. She was desperately fighting for King's attention. He called out her name, immediately she turned around.

"I'm surprised. You did a great job." he then turned to everybody.

"It's been a long morning. Everyone take a two hour lunch and come back ready to continue the day. We will be here all night."

Moneeka was burning on the inside for him. Was it love? Or the fact that she was desperate to see if she could have him? Whatever it was, she had a desire to find out. She wanted it to be something real, but if not just to shut Angie's mouth up. She knew in her heart that every man wanted her. At least that's what she thought. As everyone began to disperse King walked over to his trailer, which was next to hers. There he saw her waiting to speak with him.

"Listen, I would like to apologize for my tardiness, and... my comment about your car. It was childish." King had a blank expression on his face. He was taken aback at her proper speaking. He too had judged her like she judged him, off mere appearance.

"It's all good. May be you judged me right, maybe not. But hey everybody can change." he said smiling, as he opened the door to his trailer.

"Can we start over? Maybe go to lunch?" Moneeka asked politely.

"I'm not going out. I'ma take a shower and prepare for the next scene."

Once again she had been turned down by him. She frustratedly walked into her trailer. "Angie," she called out but got no answer. Her feelings were crushed. However, she refused to give up. Moneeka finally realized what she wanted and was determine to get it. With her same blue and white shorts on, she headed over to King's trailer. She knocked on the door but got no answer. She turned the knob and walked in. She heard the shower running and called out his name, just above a whisper. "King." At that moment she took it upon herself to go after what she thought she wanted. Hesitantly, she stepped out of her short and tossed her t-shirt to the floor and opened the shower door. To her surprise she may have bargained for more than she could handle. King was hung like a mule. Moneeka eyes widened.

She hadn't had a man's penis in her vagina in years. And from the look of it, she was wishing she didn't have to start with King. Needless to say, she wasn't about to back down. She had reached the point of no return.

Moneeka walked up to him and placed a kiss on his lips. However, he didn't move. Gently she kissed his neck making her way down to his chest. King titled his head back allowing the water to run down on her head as she went lower. Slowly, she made her way down to his enlarged penis. For a moment she didn't know what to do. She begun, kissing a- round the head of his shaft holding it with both hands. Being that his penis was the largest she had ever seen, Moneeka admired the view nervously.

Finally her tongue grazed the head of his penis, as she open her mouth taking in just a little. The back of King's head laid against the shower wall, as his body stiffened slightly from her touch. She took part of his shaft in and out of her mouth, she began to loosen up, as she got in the rhythm. Moneeka closed her eyes as she continued to suck on him, twisting his penis with every stroke as she began to have an orgasm from the pleasure she was giving him.

"Muummm," she moaned in the process. "Awww..." She squeezed out.

Finally King raised her up by the shoulders gently and kissed her passionately. Slowly, he inserted himself inside of her wetness, as she took a deep breath, holding it speechlessly.

"Woooo.." she released. King's penis was too much for her. Too much for any woman that wasn't having sex three or four times a day. Little did Moneeka know, King had only inserted the head of his penis in her. He picked her up placing both of her legs in his forearms. That's when he slid all the way in to her tightness.

With no hesitation she quickly jumped out of his arms. She looked him in his eyes, "Please take me to your bed. It's been a very long time for me."

King saw the sincerity in her eyes.

Nervously she trembled as she lay back on his bed; again he entered her, but took his time. King wasn't a dawg to just hurt her, plus he had wanted her for a while. So he made love to her.

Moneeka cried out in pain mixed with pleasure. "King, muumm ...ahhh..."

His only thought was of how tight she was...but also how good she felt to him.

POP! "Ohhh...." she moaned, as she opened all the way up, and King went deeper into her hot love oven. "Let me get on top, please." She begged.

He rolled over, as she climbed, onto him and slowly eased down on his rock hard love muscle, until it was all the way in her again. She placed her right hand on her stomach, and her left hand on his leg. "King, you're in my stomach..." Moment later she was riding him like a jockey riding a horse in the Kentucky Derby. With every thrust she yelled out, "Yes..oh yes! I've waited for this all my life!" Tears poured down her cheeks, like never before. King looked confused, but never did he stop gripping her ass.

King rolled her over and took his time, as Moneeka nails dug into his back, their eyes finally met in the heat of the moment. Again tears rolled down the side of her face. This was the feeling she had longed for, for many years. Snake never put it down on her like that.

'I'ma put it down, you gon' fall in love' Brandy's new song came to her mind and she realized that King just put it down on her and she had just fallen in love.

"Uh..." King jerked, as he released on her stomach.

She looked at him as to say, "Damn, why not in me?"

B'Shone

CHAPTER 12 Rumors

Big O and Lil Dillin pulled into the driveway of the trap house, and hopped out of the Rover, as three of the Robinson's Boyz goons exited the house with their Mack 11's in hand, preparing to leave.

"How has everything been looking around here?" O asked one of the goons.

"Quiet." He responded, "Them suckas up the street has been doing their thangs, but kept their dawg on us. I wanted to bust at that ass." He stared down the street frowning. "I sho' wish you would give us the okay to knock they fuckin' noodle loose!"

"Don't trip. As long as they don't send trouble our way we gravy baby." O said, stepping in the house.

"Ah Big O," the goons snapped his finger as if he just remembered something important. "Oh yeah. Word on the street is that King is the one supplying you and your nephew again."

Big stood there confused; he knew that was some bad information floated around the streets. He had to find away to end the rumor. If word got back to his brother he would have O's head. He knew that his brother wanted no parts of the game ever again. Big O thought about the prison stint they just did, and how his brother tried to convince him not to make the deal. Needless to say, King wasn't about to allow his brother to go at it alone.

"Who, and where the fuck did you hear that shit from?" O was fuming.

"We was at Church's Chicken, and I overheard a couple heavy weights talkin' outside, and one of them cat's name was, King Ken. And the other one was this nigga everybody call him, Big Cool-Aid. I don't know much about him but he's s'pose to be rolling out in Black Haven."

"I know Ken. I'm holla at him. He's from the Haven, and the Subs.

So I'll see where they got that info from. And see who this Cool Aid nigga is." O stated.

"Yeah, one of them said something to the fact that they can't wait to talk to King." The goon said. "Dude wants to be down wit' the fam."

He paused and looked at Big O's demeanor. "Then went on to say y'all better be ready for this cat he's been robbing and killing the big boys."

" A'ight, I got an idea who they talkin' bout. I'll handle it."

Big O strongly stated, looking at Lil Dillin. Lil Dillin was highly disappointed with the news. He knew his uncle was not going to be happy with his name being tied to some drug ring. And, in a bad way. Why? Especially associated with heroin. He was a coke dealer, never heroin. King knew all too well how much heat that shit would bring. Someone had to pay.

He looked out at Big O angrily.

"Man, we fuckin' Unk, name up out here in these streets. He'd worked too hard to clean his shit up to have us fuck it up for him again. Unk is a rich nigga without this shit." Lil Dillin paced in the driveway.

"We need to hurry up and clean this shit up, fo' he get home. He worked hard man to make us legit. Now look how we repay him."

"Nephew. You know I'll never put my brother in harm's way." Dillin looked upside O's head frowning. "That was only one time, I got this."

A couple of days had past, and the company was still going strong.

And the trap house was jumping. Big O and the goon squad went out to Club Flirt to stunt and have a good time. They had made all the money they owed Lil Paul and was now celebrating. Things couldn't have been better.

Big O found out who started the rumor and brought it to an end. King Ken was now a part of the family, and Cool Aid, they hadn't had a chance to talk to him yet, or even find out who he was.

That Friday night a car pulled into the driveway of O's trap house and then pulled right out and slowly rolled down the street, that's when he spotted Kelly P and crew posted up doing their thang. He pulled over and asked Kelly P. "Say, lil homie. You seen King?"

"Naw, what's up?" Kelly P asked, looking inside the man's car.

"I was just trying to catch, King, so I can get a half of thang. He told me he was gonna be ova here tonight." The stranger paused, "I guess he meant one of his boys was gonna be ova here. You got it?"

"I...I—gotgotcha." Kelly eyes lit up. "Pull ova, and gi...give me a cou...couple minutes."

The stranger pulled over in his CL6 and parked in front of Malcolm's trap house. Kelly P rushed in the house and forced out to Malcolm that one of Big O's people pulled up on him and asked to buy a half of kilo of heroin.

Malcolm was hesitant, but decided to question Kelly P. "So you sayin' that this nigga stopped you right?" Malcolm had enough problem with St. Louis Black and didn't need any more.

"Yeah..."

"If this shit bring trouble our way, nigga I'm chop ya' fuckin' head off." He gave it to him and said, "I don't give ah fuck what that fat ass nigga is charging but I want 50 stacks for mines." He sniffed, and wiped his nose. Kelly quickly rushed out of the house and next door to their duplex and signaled for the stranger to come on in.

A few of Malcolm's soldiers came in behind the stranger and closed the door. One stood at the door, and the others were posted in the living room and at the back door. They were ready for any sudden moves.

Kelly P sat the heroin on the table as the stranger opened up his brief case in the direction of the dope. Kelly looked on at the money with glistening eyes. The stranger looked on at the dope diligently.

"Same price?" The stranger asked.

"I don't know what, King, charges but he let us charge what we want to. And my price is fi..fi.fifty five." Without saying another word the stranger commence to counting out the money, which didn't take long due to he had all the money in five thousand dollars stacks.

"So what they call ya'?" The stranger asked Kelly P.

"They ca...ca...calll meeee...KP." he forced out.

"And you?"

"Big Cool Aid." he said placing the dope in his brief case. "Have one of ya' mans to walk me out." Kelly P nodded. "From now on I'll just stop right here and holla at cha. Cool?"

Kelly P stood there and smiled, "Cool yo...you can hit me at th...th...this number right here." Kelly P hands Cool-Aid his cell number.

Greed had gotten him. Cool-Aid opened his briefcase back up and placed the number in it. But before closing it he asked Kelly P again.

"This is, King's, dope right?" Kelly P shook his head saying yes.

"At least the same quality." Again Kelly P shook his head yes.

Cool-Aid jumped back in his Benz and drove off. Before turning on Chelsa he picked up his phone and called his people. "It's done. It's official. King's running the 1300 block again." Cool-Aid listened to his boss talking as he continued to drive up Chelsa Ave, turning on Hollywood Blvd. "I have everything on video." He smiled, "Yeah the briefcase trick did it again. I had it ready to record every time I opened it up. One of King's runners name KP sold it to me, and said it was Kings. I got it all." Cool-Aid placed his phone on speaker as he rolled him a blunt.

"Great work, Detective. We knew it was just a matter of time before he would jump back in the game. Once a hustler, always a hustler." Cool-Aid's Captain said. "This time I'm taking down the entire 1300 block!"

Captain Prewitt said excitedly. "No-one will get away this time. Not even his bad ass nephew or his brother. They're going with him. There will be no-one to take the Kin-Pin charge this time."

CHAPTER 13 Drama

"Mal," St Louis Black called out his name, "When you gonna get me my money?" he asked over the phone. He had given Malcolm 2O kilos of heroin and, he, started procrastinating on paying him. It's been over three months and every time Black came to town to collect, his money Malcolm dodged him, by not answering his calls. However, on this day Black used his main man Scooter phone.

After King gave Malcolm the 1300 block of Hyde Park, he started feeling himself. He felt that the small timer he was dealing with couldn't supply him fast enough; therefore, he searched for a new plug. St. Louis Black. Malcolm was moving 20 keys a week and it all went to his head. He actually thought of himself as being the 'Don'.

He partied, tricked off with the young hood rats- who thought he was a Don, and brought cars, jewelry, and stunted at all major events. Until, he started taking L's. His first lost came when he allow Katrice Gillespie, to trick him. She could get money from the best of them.

She was the baddest dick sucker the city ever had. She was so cold that she made Jamie Foxx write a song about her, after a one night extravaganza. Katrice played under Malcolm and talked him into going down to Tunica Casino's, where he gave her twenty grand to blow.

She was the ultimate, bona fide money go getta'. And he lost two hundred and twenty grand himself at the poker table.

"I'ma get ya' lil money!" he shouted, "Don't be sweatin' me nigga!"

Black simply laughed, "All so you ah killa now, huh?" Little did Malcolm know, Black was in town and was parked directly in his driveway. Malcolm's luxury three story mansion made him feel invincible.

This was his second down fall. Malcolm had embedded it in his head that he was the black Scar face. He had the mansion, the girls, cars and the dope, which he was snorting on the regular. Needless to say, the $1.5 million dollar mansion was now in foreclosure.

"You sure you wanna talk to me like that?" Black asked.

"What the fuck you gonna do!" Malcolm screamed into the phone, as he paced his bedroom. "I'm sick of you threaten me! I'm Alabama Muthfuckin' Malcolm! Bitch!" he stressed. "If you want it, bring it."

At that moment Black looked to the left and gave his man Scooter the go ahead. No-one ever suspected Scooter to be a killa due to him being a well respected barber, whom all the kids and parents loved. Unbeknownst to anyone, he was a real assassin.

Scooter and Tricky jumped out of the E XT and released hell on Malcolm's home. Boom, Boom, Boom, Tat, tat, tat, pop, pop, pop, zzp, zzp,zzp. Black and his crew unleash a tirade of bullets through his windows and walls. CRASH! BING! SLASH! was all Malcolm heard before hitting the floor, and crawling into his master bedroom closet where he had a secret passage way that led him down to his basement, where he had another secret exit that took him under ground to a safe house, a couple of blocks over.

Still holding on to his phone he placed it to his ear, "So that's how it's gon' be? You wanna play rough?" he changed his voice to Scarface.

He was so full of cocaine that he never thought about death. He literally thought he was Tony Montana. "Okay, now we go to war! You muthafucka you! Now you neva get pay! I'll sho' ya! You black St Louis Punk! Ok!"

St Louis Black waved for his crew to get back into the car. He was sure someone in this prestigious neighborhood had called the cops. He calmly stated with his baby boy voice, "You can run, but you can't hide. I'm well connected in this city." Black paused; he knew where Malcolm's trap houses where located. It was just a matter of time before he put an end to the fake Tony Montana's life. His days were numbered.

Malcolm ended the phone call as he continued to make his way down the tunnel to his next spot. He tripped over a log that was laying on the floor and looked back nervously, thinking that Black may be coming.

Sweating profusely, he wiped sweat from his forehead. He slowly stuck his head up out of his hiding place a couple of block over and realized that the coast was clear. Malcolm quickly hopped into his old utility van and drove to where he felt safe. The block.

"Woo...damn. I was scared as a muthfucka'. He was really trying to kill a pimp." As he pulled up on the block he stayed in the van until his soldiers came with their choppers and surrounded him. Which brought him his third lost.

Malcolm started snorting coke with a few of his crew members and every jump off in town. He also paid whatever they asked. They all came running. Some of the freaks he slept with, some he snorted with, the others he let his crew run through. Life as he knew it was one big party. Malcolm could not control his money, or his dick.

He exite the van wearing black shades, a black khaki cargo suit, black Memphis fitted baseball cap, and some black air force ones, as he tried to be incognito.

As he made it to his safe house he looked at his soldiers. "Hey!" he screamed, "That, St. Louis Black, nigga and me just had a shoot out!

I damn near killed that nigga!" Malcolm lied. He walked over to Kelly P. and wrapped his arms around him. "I need ya' baby. You gotta hold shit down fo' me. I'ma lay low and BAM!" Malcolm shouted, as Kelly P. jumped back. "I'ma take his black ass out, and then start buying work from Big O, fat ass and BAM!" again Kelly P was the only one to jump. "I'ma kill him too. Then the block would be mine. Hell the whole city would be mines!" He raised his arms high above his head as he pranced around in circles, until he heard a loud knock on the door. BOOM,BOOM,BOOM,. Malcolm dove on the floor crawling behind the couch.

"Kill'em, kill'em, kill'em!" he screamed, "that's Black, out there shooting!" All his soldiers stared on at him with a disappointed look

90

on their face.

"It's the door, dawg." one of his soldiers said.

Kelly P peeped out and smiled, "It's...it...it's fo' me." He opened the door and invited his guess into the trap.

B'Shone

CHAPTER 14 Tell Da Truth

"Our flight to, New York City, will be landing in five minutes." The flight attendant announced over the loud speaker. "Please turn off all electronic devices, and return your seat to its upright position. Also be sure to buckle in." the young attendant said politely. "And thank you for flying, Delta Express."

Moneeka and Angie exited the plane and headed directly to baggage claim. Reaching baggage claim there stood a tall 6'2 white male holding a sign that read: 'Moneeka Folks'. Moneeka had been so quiet and in a daze that she walked right past the chauffeur.

"Mo', get ya' head out of ya' ass." Angie said, "You walked right pass the driver." She turned around and pointed at the man with the black suit on, holding the sign. "Now don't tell me you didn't see his tall ass?" Angie knew the reason Moneeka had been so quiet. She wasn't used to any man turning her prissy-ass down. Every since their first day on set, Moneeka had been very distant.

Angie chimed in, "Look I know you hate what you said to the director before you found out that his fine ass was the director, but..." Before Angie could finish with her statement the chauffeur walked up to them.

"Are you Mrs. Folks, the writer?"

"That's, Ms. and yes, I am." Moneeka smiled, as the driver took her luggage.

"Your limo is right this way."

On the ride both ladies sat in silence. Angie was getting frustrated and decided to get it off of her chest. "Ya' ass ain't gon' never change. You still the same. Whenever, you can't have your muthafuckin' way you pout like"

"Shut the fuck up, Angie."Moneeka said, with a smirk. "Let me continue to enjoy my moment."Angie leaned over toward the left side of her and frowned.

"Excuse me, Ms. Bitch!"

"Oh my gosh. If you must, me and King, is cool."

Angie's eyes brows raised, "What do you mean cool?" she wanted to know all the details.

"I apologized; damn." she had gotten a little agitated, "and..." she said quickly, "I sucked his dick three days ago."

"Bitch, what you say? Don't try and talk fast now!"

A sight of relief came upon Moneeka's face. She wanted to tell Angie three days ago. And now was glad she finally got it out. "Girl, I been wanting to tell you, however, I knew you was going to say, 'I told you so.' And I just wasn't in the mood to hear all of that. I had to enjoy the moment. So please don't start now." Moneeka whined. "And yes you was right." she lowered her head, then turned toward Angie, "I haven't had any dick in my life in years. And now girl I think I'm in love, but I know he probably don't feel the same as I do." she paused, "Hell he's a fucking director for Gods, sake."

Angie sat there with her eyes wide, and her mouth gapping open. She was at a loss for words, which was a first. She couldn't believe what she had just heard. Her best friend had accomplished her mission and slept with the director.

"Tell me all the juicy details," Angie said as she slid closer to Moneeka. "And don't you dare leave out a damn thang!"

"Girl I wanted him to know that I was truly sorry. Girl...it hurt so bad, but felt so good." She placed her hands between her thighs as she thought about that wonderful night. Her thongs got moist, and she felt it, licking her lips.

"Damn it had to be good. You lookin' like you just came."

"Uh-huh" Moneeka softly moaned, ashamed that Angie had witness it. Moneeka blushed.

She went on and told her everything that had transpired between the two, from her apology to the point she crept into his trailer, and taking off her clothes after noticing that he was in the shower, to walking in on him seeing his long snake hanging, to wishing she never went in there.

Angie sat there being very attentive, smiling licking her lips as she listened to the live freak show, especially the part how she talked about sucking King's penis. Angie titled her head slightly to the left as her mouth opened and her tongue went in and out as if she was licking him.

"Mummm...." slipped out of Angie's mouth, as she closed her eyes.

"He was too much for me in that small shower, so I asked him to take me to his bed, and he did. Girl he made love to me so good that I lost my mind. Aww...oh my gosh. It was wonderful. Hell I'm still a little sore."

Unbeknownst to the both of them, the limo driver had the speaker on listening to their entire conversation. As he jacked his penis off.

He pulled into the Wyndham Hotel, got out and opened their door. He placed their luggage on the valet cart, then turned to shake Moneeka hand. As she felt the wetness she quickly snatched her hand back.

"Agh! What the hell?" she rubbed her hands on her jeans, looking at the driver, as he looked away.

Later that evening Moneeka was preparing for yet another book signing and this time it would be her last for the year. She prepping to make sure every person in the audience tongues would wag out of their mouth, the entire 15 minutes that she would be standing before them reading.

She wore a super tight revealing Louis Vuitton body dress that accented her body extremely well. It was short, but stylish. It stopped just a few inches from her ass. The brown and tan dress placed extra emphasizes on her breast, which sat perfectly, and it showed just enough stomach to make a man's nature rise.

She also wore her gold and tan Louis Vuitton six inch stiletto's strap around heels. Each time she put her heels on Angie would tell her that she looked as if she was saying, "Come fuck me!" She was definitely planning on shutting the book signing down. Moneeka was going to make sure everyone would be talking about this night for a long time to come.

She then placed her ruby red lip gloss on, making her lips look like a mirror. For the first time she asked Angie to introduce her. With pleasure she smiled and agreed. Angie walked to the podium switching her hips from side to side, as hard as she could. Her Gucci suit hugged her curves nicely. Angie stood there and smiled, waving her hand as if she was the guest speaker.

"Hey ya'll umm...yeah. Angie in this piece!." she said rolling her neck popping her lips. "Yeah umm, give it up fo' my home girl, Mo... Mo...Mo...Moneeka Folks!" She acted as if she was a rapper on the M.I.C. "Moneeka Folks, ya'll." Applause filled the small lobby, as one white prissy chick turned her nose to the air.

"Black folks are so ghetto." she said as she walked past Angie.

"Bitch, I'll turn those pretty blue eyes red if you say one mo' fuckin' thang!" Angie grabbed the lady by the arm. "Scary Ho'!"

Moneeka strutted across the lobby slow and seductive, waving the entire walk as she posed for a couple of pictures. Every woman in the lobby could tell that she was glowing. It was something women could see in one another. An elderly lady on the front row asked Moneeka as she stepped to the podium.

"Ms. Folks, are you in love? Or just got some dick? I can tell by the glow on your face." The crowd erupted in laughter. Moneeka blushed as she sat her book on the podium. "I'll take that as a yes." The elderly lady said. "So does that mean we won't be getting any more sex novels?" the freaky old lady asked, "Cause baby, these books help me get my freak on." She stood and started gyrating in the air while she bit down on her bottom lip.

Again the room erupted in laughter.

"I'm so glad you enjoy my novel, ma'am. And no it want be the last.

I'm just working on my movie right now, called FOOLED'. However, I also have another book coming out called, 'The Evil Side of Her' part two to this one." Moneeka paused and looked around the room and notice a woman coming in and sat at the back by herself. "That's strange." she thought.

"I would like to read to you a couple of paragraph from "Everybody Wants Her" She noticed how some opened their books, and others sat in attention.

"Starting in Chapter 14, let's see at the fourth paragraph on page 115." She directed them before starting. "Okay, Robin was now living alone and lonely. She laid in the bed in her teddy thinking of how much she hated Micole for ruining her marriage, and how weak her husband was for allowing her to enter their home. Robin had hated Shone with everything in her, but for these last couple of months she couldn't stop thinking about him.

As she looked at her recorded video over and over of their sexcapade she observed something that she never noticed before. How much he was really in to it. Up until the point where Micole played with Shone's rectum and he loved it.

And that's when she saw it. The small, hair-line scar around Micole's clitoris and another scar under her ass cheek. Robin looked even closer and notice that Shone was in Micole's ass. And she was enjoying it like it was her vagina. Robin looked confuse. She paused the video and remembered that Micole said she went to Fairly High School. But quote unquote stayed to herself. Again she played the video looking hard. That's when she paused it again. 'The eyes' Robin said. She had gotten a good look at Micole's eyes.

Quickly, Robin leaped out of her bed and rushed over to her closet and retrieved her 1990 high school year book. She looked for the name Micole Perison, but couldn't find it. That is until she seen those eyes. Robin sat back down on her bed with a devilish smirk on her face. She had found her true identity."

Moneeka paused for effect. She looked out into the crowd to see their reaction to the story, to those who had no book, sitting on the edge of their seats. One man leaped up out of his seat and ran to the back door screaming, "I gotta get me a book!" Angie stood off to the side signaling for Moneeka to continue to read. Angie had a confused look on her face.

"I have to get me a book when this shit is over." Angie stated.

Moneeka continued to read, "Robin, lept to her feet and instantly logged on to Facebook, and searched for her old classmates. She wanted to know if anyone seen Micole Perison. Startled by her phone ringing, she glanced at the caller I.D."Shone, I wonder what the hell he wants. But it was perfect timing." Robin said. "What Shone? Neva mind what you want. I have something for you. Your lover, Micole, I just wanted you to know that," Robin paused, "Naw fuck it. You'll hear about it...."

"I'm going to have to stop right here." Moneeka said.

"Awe, come on!" The elderly lady screamed. "I'm waiting for the part were, Robin, got the shit fucked out of her. That's always the good part."

"Well you'll have to finish reading it for yourselves. Because there is a lot more of that in the story. Thank you all again for coming out; I'll be in the lobby for another thirty minute autographing books." She smiled and walked toward the front. She noticed Angie looked her up and down frowning as she walked past. She knew something was terribly wrong with her friend.

CHAPTER 15 Da Come Up

"Word on the street is that, St. Louis Black is gunning for Malcolm." Big O said to the goon squad, as he paced the floor of his master suite at the Peabody Hotel. He knew the 1300 block was about to get heated up and he wanted to get his crew away from the hood for a minute or two.

St. Louis Black and King started in the game at the same time when Black's mother divorced his father and moved to Memphis, from St. Louis, Missouri when he was only 14-years-old. Upon getting in trouble over and over again, his mother had no choice but to allow him to go back and live with his father, now that he was 17. She truly didn't want to send her son back to that environment, being that she knew of her ex-husbands gangsta ways. Something she didn't want for her son. Needless to say, Black was out of control. He was too much for her to handle. Black stood 5'8" and was all muscle; blacker than train smoke and tougher than nails. Black loved to play with pistols, and his demeanor, let's just say it was calm but dangerous.

As soon as Black moved back in with his father, he allegedly shot a 24-year-old man standing on the corner of Grand and Kossuth. Rumors filled the streets that the man lived and was now seeking to kill Black. However, his father put an end to it fast. He terrorized the entire North side, which gave his son the green light for destruction.

"Also, that makes it better for us." Big O smiled, holding up a kilo of coke in his right hand, and a kilo of heroin in his left hand. "Everybody wants her," he raised his right hand higher, "And everybody wants him." He raised his left hand in reference to the heroin, or so we call it dog food.

"So what you sayin', we ain't trappin' in the 13 no mo'?" A goon asked.

"Oh yeah. I just need for everybody to stay strapped at all times." Big O tossed the dope on the counter top and firmly stated, "Although we know that they're beefin', shit rolls down hill. But we're the water hoses that gonna send it back up hill. We ain't doin' no running."

The crew cheered on as they all stood around counting money.

"But what about, King? What if he finds out?" another goon asked.

Big O knew that his brother would eventually find out, but he just wanted to make a couple more good runs before shit hit the fan. O knew that it normally took him at least two to three months to shoot those quick movies. He had another month to go. Before his brother makes it back Big O planned on having the house boarded back up. O was smart enough to call his brother twice a week to keep tabs on his where abouts.

"Before my brother makes it back, everyone in this room should be sitting pretty nice with that cash." He pointed to every man in the room. "Everyone should be at least at a half ah ticket. If not someone fucked up bad! We got the cheapest prices and the best work in the city."

Lil Dillin sat over in the far right corner looking out the window, which over looked the entire downtown area. He was not into their conversation. His mind was somewhere else. Everyone was happy about their new plug, and the money they were making. They were popping bottles and blowing on some Cush. All of a sudden they heard a knock at the door. One of the goons turned the music down, as Big O stuffed the coke and heroin in the pillows.

"Who is it?" a member of the T.B.F (Thrill Brother Family) shouted.

A squeaky voice penetrated through the thick wooden door.

"Candice." A soft sultry voice came in. Quickly O rushed over to open the door, and there she stood, Candice 'Candy' Jackson and the 901 fantasy dancers. The entire crew smiled, except Lil Dillin. O had contacted Candy and crew to come help him celebrate their new success.

The party was on. Everyone was in to it, tossing money everywhere.

Big O looked over at Dillin and couldn't figure out what was wrong.

Candy had brought five of the baddest females the city had to offer with her. Within seconds, naked women were dancing all around the place and having a great time.

Candy stood dancing to the music with an extremely short white skirt on that stopped just below her ass cheeks. She observed Lil Dillin glaring out the window not paying any attention to the party that was taking place inside the hotel room. She sashayed her way over to him and danced in front of him, exotically. He still remained in a trance. She turned her back toward him, as she bent over touching her toes, revealing her Super Woman Thong, as she stepped out of her skirt. She laid on her back spreading her legs wide open showing her pink treasure box. She looked up at him, smiled and licked her lips.

Big O stood off to the side, and couldn't help but to notice his little nephew demeanor. Dillin stood, and walked to the back bedroom and closed the door behind him. He just wasn't in the mood. Big O tossed a few more big faces in the air, and walked to the back room.

"Nephew," O said, walking into the room with a blunt the size of a mini baseball bat in his mouth, "What's the deal? You had pussy all in ya' grill and you ran back here. Hell, Tresha, ain't gonna find out 'bout this."

"Listen, Unk." Dillin stood, and paced the floor, "you said once we finish those first one hundred keys that we were finish. Now this Lil Paul, nigga just sent us, 100 keys of boy, and now 300 keys of that girl. Man do you give a fuck about ya' brother anymore?!"

"What type of question is that? He ain't got shit to do with this!"

O yelled. "We straight nigga! As long as he don't come around the 1300 the FEDS, can't tie him into this shit!" O spit.

Lil Dillin stopped pacing the floor and looked O up and down.

"Them bitches do what the fuck they wanna do! Are you crazy?!
104

Or have you forgotten? Ya' brother didn't have shit to do with the last time he went to jail! He told ya' hard headed ass not to go and fuck with that nigga, Gordin, but you did anyway! He loves you so much that he couldn't allow you to go by yourself, so he went with you, and look what happen. It was a set up!"

"I took the leadership roll!" O shouted back.

"So fuckin' what? If you would have just listened he, nor you would have done all that time! Every time, he went to jail was becuz of you. He took the charge to keep you outta jail." Dillin was pissed, "He wouldn't have a fuckin' criminal record if it wasn't for you. Just becuz he promised my grand dad that he will always take care of ya' ass!"

O sat down on the bed not saying shit. He leaned over and placed his blunt in the ashtray. He was at a loss for words. Lil Dillin had never expressed how he felt about anything; he just went along with whatever his uncles said. O knew that the word had gotten back to his older sister KeKe, Dillin's mother. She felt that nothing good was going' to come out of them selling drugs. Especially since King had everything set up for them. Money was never a problem.

Big O placed his heads in the palms of his hands, and thought about life. Greed had gotten the best of him. It was eating on his insides, and finally made its way out. For the love of money is the root of all evil. And Big O was one evil brother, when it came to money. No matter how much money he had it was never enough.

"So what ya' sayin' is to give all this shit back?" O asked.

"Naw...get rid of it, and I'm finish."

O nodded in agreement, "Unk, our block is hotter than Nevada multiplied by three. Them FEDS coming, the robbers, and...a war."

"Let's down this work and we go back to what Big Bruh laid out fo' us. Deal?" Big O stood there with his arms open widen, waiting for his nephew to embrace him. Slowly Dillin walked over.

"Deal. Now I'll go fuck that, Candy chick."

CHAPTER 16 Quick Money

"Who the hell is this, fat fuck?!" Malcolm shouted, as K.P escorted Cool-Aid into their trap house.

"This my man Cool-Aid." Kelly P introduced to the crew. There he stood, only 5'8", low fade, medium skin complexion, about 295 pounds with a dark red Polo shirt on, and a bright cool-aid smile. "He...he... the one bought that half the other day." Kelly P explained.

Malcolm scanned him up and down and notice that he was wearing a diamond-beveled Cool-Aid medallion that sat on his protruding belly, as he stood there holding his brief case in hand. Malcolm's nose began to run from the coke draining that he recently snorted. Cool-Aid remained calm, not saying a word.

"So what's up big boy? What you need?" Malcolm asked, but Cool-Aid turned his attention toward Kelly P.

"He...he straight." K.P stuttered.

"Damn right I'm straight! I'm the fuckin' boss!"

With that being said, Cool-Aid walked over to the table and opened the briefcase turning it around showing everybody in the room the money, as well as getting all of their faces on the camera. From the moment he opened it, the briefcase began recording.

"I need the same thang." He made sure to have the camera on Malcolm, due to the fact that he was snorting coke right in front of him. Over and over, he dug his pinky nail in a tube of coke and went straight to the head with it.

Malcolm instructed K.P to count the money, "And, Smurf, run next door and look in the bathroom floor board and get that brown bag, and cover everything else back up. The brown bag should be the one." He then paused and took another sniff of coke. He was so high that he couldn't stand on his own two feet without staggering.

Cool-Aid sat back and smiled. He now had enough evidence to take out King's empire— so he thought.

"Tell, King, I said thanks for looking out."

"Fuck, King! It's, Malcolm, and the soldier mob, bitch!" again he staggered. "Alabama's finest!"

"So this ain't, King's, work?" Cool-Aid asked.

"Naw, nig...ga!" At that moment all you heard was the sounds of guns being cocked. "What you don't want it?" Malcolm asked, strongly.

"Wooo.... what's all that fo'?" Cool-Aid asked, as he stared at K.P. "I can care less. As long as the price the same and the quality is still the same, I don't give a rat's ass."

"That, that that's what's up bro." K.P. chimed in.

He wanted that extra five grand since he was only making three grand a week being the lookout boy, and everyone else was making major moves.

Moments later Smurf came rushing back inside the trap house. He came back with the brown bag of heroin, sat it on the table and Big Boy smiled. "Another successful transaction." Cool-Aid thought to himself. Malcolm's crew was quick to search a person, but never a brief case full of money. Greed and stupidity had taken over the 1300 block of Hyde Park.

"I'll get up with y'all in a couple of days." Cool-Aid gave K.P. dap, as one of their soldiers walked him out to his car. As he drove off, he went up Chelsa until crossing over Hollywood Blvd, and then pulled over at Fashion Corner where he met Captain Lee Johnson.

"How did it go?" Captain Johnson asked.

"It's all good. I got names, picture, dope, and guns." He paused and gave the Captain a strange stare, "But they admitted that the dope ain't coming from, King. They got beef with each other. You remember that clown that calls himself, Alabama Malcolm?"

"So what? We gonna implement, King's crew in it all."

"Cap, maybe this, King, fellow is legit. I've found out yesterday that he's been in, Atlanta, filming a movie for the last two months."

Captain Johnson rushed into Cool-Aid's face and began to shout. "Fuck what you found out! That no good muthafucka is supplying his

109

brother and that wild ass nephew of his. I'ma get them all!" he screamed, "And you better make damn sho' that we can prove it! Now, get the fuck outta here!" he insisted as saliva jumped out of his mouth.

Cool-Aid stood there and gritted at his Captain. He knew that Captain Johnson had it in for King's family every since he found out that Big O and Lil Dillin turned his two young daughters out to selling their bodies, and King had filmed the Captain's wife fucking Mr. Marcus in a porn. He married a freak, and his daughters turned out to be hoes. Once a hoe, always a hoe. With that being said, he started drinking.

***

The entire flight, Angie didn't say two words to Moneeka. Something was eating away at her friend and it started to bother her. However, Moneeka was still floating on cloud nine. Therefore she never bothered to ask her 'what's wrong?' As they were taking a cab back to the hotel Moneeka suggested that they stop at Gladys Knight chicken and waffles on Peach Tree for something to eat.

Still no conversation occurred between the two, until a tall man walked over to the table trying to flirt with Moneeka. Angie noticed and rolled her eyes.

"Excuse me, ma'am; but don't I know you?"

Moneeka gave a friendly smile and asked, "Do you read books?"

The gentleman frowned, "No. Why you asked?"

"Then you don't know me. I'm not from here."

He was persistent, "See that's why I'm over here. I would like to get to know you."

"Sorry but I have someone."

"Pshh..." Angie hissed. Moneeka looked upside her head as the man walked away from the table.

"My gosh, Ang, what seems to be your problem? You been having a nasty attitude every since we left the book signing. What is it?"

Moneeka asked in a low tone trying not to cause a scene. "I know I couldn't have done anything that bad for you not to say what I have done."

Angie knew that she had to finish reading the book before she could make an accurate assumption about her long time friend. Every since Angie got out of the hospital 10 years ago, Moneeka had been there for her the entire way. Angie needed to finish reading the book before she snapped.

"I'm good." she quickly said rolling her eyes.

"So, why the harsh tone?"

Angie didn't want to go into details yet, so she changed the subject. "Now that we're back in, Atlanta, you gonna suck some mo' dick?" She asked being sarcastic. She truly didn't care one way or another. Her mind was on that book, but she tried to remain cordial.

"I pray girl. We haven't talked since that night. I'm so confused." Moneeka admitted, as they finished their dinner, "but before I can do that again, I'm going to need a few tips, from the master." she hit Angie on the arm. "Because every since, Snake, moved to Nashville, I haven't had a dick in my life."

"First get ya' nose out ya' ass and stop talkin' like a white ho'."

"I do not talk like a white girl, Angie." Moneeka said, as she took a sip of her ice tea.

"I know ya' a nasty ass, freaky bitch. So ya can play someone else." Angie snapped, after having a flashback. "So stop the act and suck it like you did..." she paused and looked off.

"Like what?" Moneeka asked, suspiciously, "Like what?"

CHAPTER 17 War

It was a late Saturday night and the 1300 was jumping like Beale Street. Cars lined the street from one end to another. Hookers and hoes damn near no clothes, pranced up and down the street, in search for the next trick. Customer's fiending for a hit, as they played one deal to another. Big O and the T.B.F crew had it jumping on the low end, and Malcolm's crew had it going on up top.

A black Chevy Impala, pulled around back, near the rail road tracks as three henchmen dressed in all black exited the vehicle, with choppers in hand, ready to lay the entire block down. However, just before they placed ski-mask on their faces there was a nosy bystander watching and filming everything. As they got ready to head toward the pathway that led to the block un-noticed, the lead henchman told the fourth member, to stay in the car.

"Keep it running. Be ready and keep ya' eyes open."

The three took off ducking behind any and everything they could to go un-noticed. Slowly, they came up behind Big O's trap house and surveyed the block. As they were preparing to move further on down a pit bull in the yard next to them began to bark, loudly. Again they stopped.

One of the henchmen said, "I can see that nigga from here." He whispered. "He's doing what he always do; standing in the middle of the street stunt'n. This is gonna be like taking candy from a baby."

"Fuck this." the head henchman said, "I'm sick of this shit, I'm killin' that nigga right now."

At the same time Lil Dillin was posted in the street talking to the neighborhood freak Kita Red. That's when he observed something coming away from around the house moving swiftly toward their way. His eyes were wide open when he saw the masked men with those choppers.

"Guns!" Dillin screamed, "Malcolm crew trying to creep us!" At that moment, every crew on the block started shooting. From Big O and the T.B.F. to Malcolm and his soldiers to the three henchmen. Shots rang out like the Fourth of July. Bullets flying, hookers crying, and bodies dying. It was a mini massacre on the 1300 block.

Kelly P ran and ducked behind his red Ford F250, and thought that he would go un-noticed, but one of the henchmen ran up on him, but before shooting Kelly P begged for his life.

"Fuck, Malcolm, and this block." he cried, "I got kids and a wife, and I have 150 large in the glove compartment of this truck." Kelly P hit the right front finder of the truck.

"I hate a coward. Fuck ya'!" POW! POW! Two shots to the head.

Big O notice another one of the henchmen creeping up behind Lil Dillin, who was posted up alongside a large tree shooting his 40 cal.

"Thunder Caaaaaat!" O yelled, "Get down!" at the same time Big O was aiming his pistol in the direction of the henchman, giving him a bullet to the back of his skull, but not before he released two into Lil Dillin's chest, as he fell to the ground and instantly started gagging on his blood. O raced over to Dillin side. That's when the two remaining henchmen retreated to their get-a-way vehicle. Big O jumped to his feet with his nephew in his arms heading straight for his Range Rover, placing Dillin on the back seat, and sped off to the MED.

Malcolm, and his few remaining soldiers quickly dispersed as they all got in their cars leaving the scene. Siren could be heard coming. Needless to say fiends still walked around looking for a hit.

***

Driving as fast as he could, and running every light on Poplar, Big O called his big sister, Keke. Something he would later regret.

"Big Sis," O said breathing heavily dodging traffic. "Meet me at the MED," he paused when he heard her gasp for air, "Thunder Cats...been shot."

Her scream and cry was heard echoing through the phone by another T.B.F. member riding in the back holding Lil Dillin's head. O hung up the phone and looked back at Dillin. "Hold on nephew, I'm pulling up to the door now." Quickly he hopped out of his SUV and rushed into the hospital screaming, "Help, help, help! I need some help!"

A doctor ran over to him, with a couple of EMT's.

"What's wrong, son?" An older white doctor asked.

"He's in the truck." was all O managed to let come out of his mouth.

The doctor and the emergency crew rushed out to Big O's Rover and got Dillin and immediately rushed him into surgery. It wasn't looking good for him and O knew it.

O stood there with tears of anger in his eyes.

***

"I'ma kill that fat Muthafucka!" Malcolm loudly stated, as he hit the steering wheel while driving toward the Marriot Hotel, on Perkins and I-240. He was livid. "I should have followed my mind the first day he bought his ugly ass back on my block! They killed my main men! K.P. and Lil Smurf!" Again Malcolm banged on the steering wheel. Tears trickled down his face, out of frustration. "I'ma kill'em! They want, live to see the sun go down tomorrow! I promise ya' that! I'ma get revenge for my crew!" he cried to his new lieutenant in charge.

He pulled into the Marriot Hotel parking lot, and gave him instructions to go get a couple of rooms for the night. As his lieutenant hopped out of the car, Malcolm leaned over to his glove compartment and retrieved a small chap stick tube full of coke and took a sniff.

"Wow...sniff, sniff" He raised his head up and looked into the rear view mirror and wiped his nose. Again he thought he was Tony Montana, "Okay, now we go to war! You fat fuck!"

***

"Get those indictments ready." Captain Johnson firmly stated to his secretary. "Contact the, Judge and let him know that within the last two months we have purchase over three kilos of heroin from the 1300 block of Hyde Park, and we have everything on tape." He paused, thinking of what else to say, "Also, now as he can see for himself as he turned on the news that they just went to war over some damn drugs! We have nine dead bodies being carried to the morgue on the count of that drug infested block." He then turned to his other officers in his department.

"I want every dealer and killer associated with the 13." Captain Johnson had the ATF, the FEDS, OCU (Organize Crime Unit) MPD (Memphis Police Department), and the Western District Task Force, aiming to take down the 1300 block. Enough was enough.

Quickly, he turned to Cool-Aid, "Make damn sure you get King and his brother. His nephew is probably dead by now. That's one less T.B.F. member I'll have to worry about."

"Yes sir, Captain." Cool-Aid said, as he turned to exit the station. He reached into his pocket and got his cell phone. "Yeah it's me. It's just like you said it would be. Shit bout' to hit the fan fo' err'body." He paused and listened. "Okay, one. Talk to you later, and check, out Wing City, you'll find someone sitting there drinking."

***

Keke stood over her son's body crying uncontrollably. She couldn't stand all the tubes running throughout his frail body. It was more than her nervous heart could take. She felt that his life was coming to an end the moment he started back selling drugs. Lil Dillin was her only child and there was nothing she, as a mother, could do now to protect him from the dangers of this world. Keke looked at Big O who was on the phone. Hatred for her brother entered her heart. She knew it was all his fault. Keke turned and walked out of the room. She got on her cell phone and made a call. "Hello" she cried, "Lil Dillin is in the hospital fighting for his life and I don't think," she paused, "Well the doctors said it don't look good for him." She listened to the person on the other end. "His fat ass in there on the phone like he don't have a care in the world." Again she listened, "Wait. How did you find out so quickly? Did he call you?" She wiped her eyes, "Okay I'll be here until you show up. I'ma make sho' he don't take his ass nowhere! O ain't no damn fool to leave now. He'll be here."

CHAPTER 18 Da Med!

"Hey, King." said Moneeka, seductively as she walked on the set and stood beside him, as he hung up his cell phone, revealing a frustrated expression on his face; a look of disappointment. King never noticed her presence as she stood next to him. He was preparing to walk off the set until she discreetly, rubbed his hand. "King." again she softly spoke.

"Is everything alright?" Still in a trance, he turned around and snatched his arm away from her. Frightened, Moneeka jumped back and saw redness in his eyes, as of fire.

Slowly, she backed away. Finally, he snapped back to reality.

"I'm sorry. My mind was somewhere else." King said, "I have an emergency back in Memphis that I have to go tend to." He tried to walk off. "I'll call you later."

Again she walked back up to him and glanced over her shoulder making sure that no-one was watching. She took his hand, and as she tried her best to conceal her love for him and to keep the cast member out of her business, she said "I'm going to go back with you for support."

"Naw, you have to finish filming this movie. It wouldn't be good for your career to walk out on a movie." he looked her in the eyes.

Quickly she responded, "I only have one last scene to complete and it's over for me." She pleaded to him. She wanted badly to be next to the man she had fallen head-over-hills for.

"My plane leaves within the next couple of hours, so if you get finish, I'll see you at the airport. If not I'm out." He turned and headed out to his car, making a mad dash for the hotel.

Moneeka desperately wanted to be a part of whatever it was King had going. She was willing to sacrifice her career, if not for anything other than comfort.

Moneeka felt for a quick minute that it was only about the sex with him. She felt low. "Did I just give him all I had just to be thrown back to the wolves?" she asked herself. She had begun to feel that she was just another one night stand to him; another notch in his belt of groupies. A sadden look graced her face.

From a distance, Angie stood back and observed what had just taken place. She felt a little sympathy; however, she was still upset about Moneeka's book. She smartly looked away.

**

"I'm in the air heading to Memphis. I should be touching down within the next 30 minutes." He listened to his partner on the other end of the phone, as the stewardess placed a glass of Crown Royal on his fold out tray that was stationed in front of him.

"Will that be all?" asked the Stewardess.

He nodded yes, with the phone still to his right ear. "No that's aight. I left my car at the airport, so I'll be there as soon as I touch down." King hung up, downed his drink then laid his head back and closed his eyes. King knew the moment he left his brother wasn't going to do right and that's why he called and old friend to keep everything in prospective.

***

King pulled up in front of Wing City, on Airway Blvd, and got out the car. "I'll be right back. Just sit here. The three wise men don't talk around people their not familiar with." He entered the restaurant and walked down the stairs into the basement where he saw the three wise men sitting - John Ward, (Owner) Willie Hardamen, (Mississippi Playboy) and Bob Winbush, (Mr. Information).

He entered their presence, and stood there and waited for one of them to tell him to take a seat. They knew why King was there. They also knew that he had been out of the game for more than10 years. They also knew that it was bad for his name out in the streets. King needed info and he was at the right place. The three always kept their ear to the streets.

At that moment a young tender came in with four glasses and a fifth of Remy Martin V.S.O.P. and bent over placing it on the coffee table.

The mini skirt she wore was definitely a mini. It revealed her god-given assets and a firm round back side. Being that all the wise men were in their 60's, they wanted nothing old but money. The young tender sat on Willie lap after he slapped her on the ass and said with

121

his raspy voice, "Now that's a nice piece of ass, boy." he looked at King, "take a seat."

"Okay, Son, wha'cha wanna know?" Ward asked.

King lowered his head, "Who shot my, nephew?" he was hurting. Lil Dillin was the only nephew he had and losing him wasn't good for anyone. He raised his head.

"Just being straight up wit'cha," Ward said placing his hand in front of him, "Son, the missing pieces to the puzzle been wit'cha all along."

"I'm confused." King frowned, looking at the three. "What do you mean?"

Winbush chimed in, "Your new chick holds the key to ya' ansa'."

King scratched his head and added, "She was in Atlanta with me."

Again Willie raspy voice kicked in, as he continued to rub the young tender on the ass, "You ain't as bright as I thought you were."

King turned to John Ward again, "Son, ya' brother been selling dope again."

"I know." King replied.

"You know, Malcolm didn't like the fact that ya' brother was back on the block that you gave him. So there was tension." Ward explained calmly. "Plus, St Louis Black, had beef with Malcolm; and since ya' brother started back dealing he was taking money out of Black's squad mouth." Ward took a sip of his Remy.

122

"Plus," the raspy voice eased in, "you had those robbers trying to get a quick come up."

"So, Malcolm, Black, and the robbers? But my chick is the key?"

"I didn't say she was the key, but she holds the key." Winbush repeated. "If you could get her to tell you about her girlfriend, then you can get the answers that you're searchin' for."

King nodded as he stood to exit the private party. "Thanks." He reached into his inside jacket pocket and pulled out ten racks and dropped it on the coffee table. Before exiting the room Willie asked, "How did you know ya' brother was back in the game?"

"I was taught by the best." King winked and walked out.

On the ride to the hospital King thought about what the three wise men had said, 'Your girl holds the key.' He continued to ponder that statement over and over in his head.

"Did you get everything you needed?" his passenger asked.

He looked, and nodded yes. He felt that the three wise men blessed him with the tools he needed to locate the assassin. "From here on out, I have to make my every move a calculated step."

Moments later King turned onto the parking lot of the Med Hospital.

He strolled through the sliding double glass doors, and approached the receptionist desk. He glanced to the right of him, and noticed a couple of his old henchmen in the gift shop. King gave a slight head nod.

"Can you please tell me what room is Alex Dillin, is in?" King asked.

Immediately, the receptionist entered the name in the computer that was at her desk. There she searched until finding his name. "Here we go. He's in room 901." Slowly she looked up at King, "Sir right now it's family only, and"

"I am family." King strongly stated and walked off.

King and his guest stepped off the elevator and noticed that the entire T-B.F. crew was stationed throughout the 9th floor lobby. He witnessed Tresha and KeKe crying their hearts out all over dirty money. He walked past them all, not saying a word and entered room 901.

What he saw made him take a couple of steps backward. He could not believe his eyes. Tears streamed down his face like never before, but nothing came out of his mouth. Dillin had more tubes running in and out of his body than a car engine with wires. Rage, anger, and revenge blessed his face. King mouthed, "I'm killin' every party involved."

Snoring penetrated his ears, as he quickly glanced over to the window and saw his brother lying on the couch sleep. Instantly, he rushed over to him, grabbed him by his collar as he was preparing to hit him, Big O woke up.

"Bruh, what the fuck is wrong wit' you?" Being that O was bigger than his brother King had a wrestle on his hand. He mashed O's head against the window and shouted.

"Look at what the fuck you have caused our family!" he spent him around while he remained holding his brother in a chock whole. "This shit is your fault!" Moneeka rushed into the room, and seeing King and O tangled up and rushed over to help him, by hitting O in the face. King Let him go and turned to Moneeka and screamed at her.

"Get the fuck out!" Moneeka had seen him in a light like never before. With that being said, she quickly turned and rushed out. She bumped into Keke and a few of the crew as they tried to make their way in the small room. Again he shouted, "OUT!"

After all the commotion between the two brothers died down everyone entered the room again but no-one said a word. They didn't want to be a part of that feud. King wanted badly to make his brother trade places with his nephew, but he loved his brother just as much. He turned and walked out, and Moneeka quickly followed behind him.

***

Driving up Union Ave, King looked at Moneeka, "You can stop all that damn crying!" He shouted, "You were right about me. I ain't shit but a common thug! That's what you thought right? So now you see." He was livid. "Well if you stick around any longer you will get a chance to see my gansta side. So my advice to you is, get the fuck on with your life!" He picked up his cell phone and called an old killer.

"Big Run? How soon can you get in that Cutlass and meet me at Top's Bar-B-Q on Jackson and Watkins?" King asked.

Runn sensed the tension in his tone. "I'm around the corner."

"I'm waitin'."

He pulled into Top's and looked at Moneeka. "You wanna be down with me?"

She nodded, "Yes." while wiping her face.

"Then what's your girlfriend's name, and where do she stay?"

Frighten she answered, "Who Angie?"

"I don't know the bitch! The one you're with all the time."

"She's at home." she said looking out the window. "You remember she was on the plane with us. She took a taxi to the house."

"And her address is?"

At that moment Big Runn pulled onto the parking lot.

"Neva mind, you're going with us." he open the door, "Come on! King took her by the arm as they hopped into Runn's car.

CHAPTER 19 Game Ova

"Dawg, you can't continue to drink like this. This shit ain't good for your health." One of Big O's goons informed him, after walking into his home looking at him, and the terrible conditions. The house reeked with a horrible odor, whiskey bottles everywhere, dishes in the sink, and he hadn't changed clothes for days. He was truly taking his nephew being shot serious. He was letting him-self go down to the dogs.

Every since he seen his nephew laying on his death bed, fighting for his life, and his brother not talking to him any longer, O didn't care about life anymore. All of his demons were haunting him, which drove him down that road of destruction -- drinking. His love for the game was over.

O stood and staggered over to his bar and knocked all the bottles to the floor. "Ahgggg!" he screamed out. Big O looked around his luxurious home at all the amenities he had accumulated. Four 85 inch flat screens, new pool table, theater room; he had it all. Big O even took up all the hard wood floors in his home and had one hundred dollar bills sprinkled throughout the entire house on the floors, and had a clear mold of plastic laid across the money and sealed which added up to twenty eight thousand dollars on the floors to walk on. O had the money to blow.

Big O stumbled over to the patio door, slid it open and stepped out onto it. He looked around his back yard admiring the view, then at his pool which was shaped into a dollar sign. Illegal money had gotten the best of him. He stood there and took in all the fresh air he could before vomiting. Carmichael, his right hand man rushed to his aid.

"Big man you aight?"

O leaned over with both hands on his knees, glanced up, "I'm good." He breathed heavy. "I needed that." O said wiping a big glob of saliva that hung from his mouth, along with food particles. "I'm done."

"With what?" Carmichael asked.

O stood and walked back into the house and plopped down on his couch, and reached for his cell phone. "The game." While dialing he said, "Fuck this shit. It ain't worth it anymore." He placed the phone to his ear, then pulled it away, placed it on speaker and sat it on the table. He wanted his man to hear everything that he was about to say. He wanted a witness to verify the decision he was making. The phone rang three times before he heard a deep voice.

"Big Baby, what it do?" The man on the other end said cheerfully.

"It's bad, Lil Paul." O replied.

"You tellin' me. I heard about nephew. Is he gonna be alright?"

"It's hard to tell at this moment. He's fucked up bad."

"Ya'll have my deepest sympathy." Paul said.

"Listen, Paul." O said, as he took a deep breath, "I'm done my man."

"Already." Paul said excitedly, "The moving truck will be there first thing in the morning."

"NO!" Big O shouted, "Nigga I'm finish! Done! Ova wit'! I'm out the game! When my people get finish, I'ma send you your money and I'm done!"

"Damn, Big Man. You out cuz of ya' nephew. Playa, that's part of the game."

O was fueled with anger. He loved his nephew with all he had, and to hear those comments come from Paul's mouth made him even madder.

"Nigga, what part of the game is this? When ya' family fighting for their life, and the only brother you have don't want to have shit to do with you! Nigga this ain't the part I signed up for! So fuck you and the game!" Big O wasn't a coward by far. He didn't give a fuck about Paul getting mad. The love for his family was more important to him than anything. "Nigga we were millionaires before I brought my stupid ass up there to fuck with that bitch, and you! I fucked up! Not him! I dragged him into the game! He didn't ask for this shit!"

"I told you that your brother would find out." Paul remained calm. "And I also told you, that the game ain't the same. And that you would have to watch your steps. And…" Paul paused, "I also told you nigga," he voice changed to frustrated, "that we was in this shit to the end! And the end ain't here yet. Unless I say it's the end!"

129

"It is what it is." O stated strongly.

"Okay. Get me my money nigga." Click. Paul hung up.

***

Angie rushed out of Barns and Nobel, hopped into her car racing home. She was in dire need to read Moneeka's book. She even ran two red lights trying to make it home. Upon seeing the police pulling out of a Circle K she slowed her car down. At that moment her phone rang. Reaching into her purse she pulled it out looking at the caller I.D. She smiled. It was Montrell, her ole lover, and owner of Montrell's barber shop.

"Heyyyy, Montrell." Angie said, seductively. She had always loved him despite the fact that he wouldn't marry her when she was ready to settle down and get re-married, after her big ordeal. However, she respected him for being a listening ear, and never judging her. And the fact that he was a shoulder for her to cry on, in her time of need. She always had a special place in her heart for him.

"What's good, ma'." Montrell's deep voice rang through the phone.

"Nut'n, headin' home."

"You still fuckin' wit' old boy, Bo?" Montrell asked out of concern.

Angie was thrown aback by the question. He never questioned her about any man she ever dated. When he called, it was a straight booty call; a real freak session. Which she was freely and willingly to give to

130

him at any time. Montrell was a real street dude, he would never mention BOBO's name unless something was seriously wrong.

"Yeah, why?" she asked.

"Listen. I ain't hatin' on ol' boy, but uummm you need to just be careful. You my girl and I just want you to know that ol' boy fuckin' with somebody that is fuckin' everybody. Except me. I don't want it at all! I've heard all the rumors about this person. And me and you fuck around that's why I'm tellin' you this shit. I need for that pussy to stay cool. I'm just keepin' it real wit' cha. So you might want to keep it P.G. wit' that nigga." Montrell was only trying to save his home girl life, and his own as well.

He went to the clinic after he witnessed BoBo interact with the chick that day at his shop. They both were sleeping with fire head Angie.

His check-up was clean; he wanted Angie's to be the same way.

Montrell went on and told Angie the stranger's name. She gasped for air. She knew the rumors about the stranger were true, but never did she think that BoBo would fuck with her. Angie never suspected that it would come so close to home.

"Thanks, Montrell." her heart sunk in her chest. She was saddened. Angie felt that everybody she trusted or gave her heart to had stepped on it; betrayed her. Why?

"I've always been real with everybody. But to have another woman come in and take another one of my men...she can have him, but it would be in a pine box. I'm gonna kill this one." She told

131

herself.

Rushing into her home Angie called out BoBo's name. "BOBO!" but her calls went unanswered. Again she called out his name, "BOBO!" but still no answer. She quickly pivoted on her heels and turned and walked into the bathroom. Empty. She stood in the bathroom doorway and reached into her pocket for her I-Phone, only to find out that it was dead. Quickly she ran into the kitchen and grabbed her house phone off the counter; at the same time plugging up her cell phone.

She called BoBo's phone but got no answer. "Ahggg!" she screamed, it went straight to his voice mail. She refused to leave a message; she wanted to talk to him face to face. She was determined to get to the bottom of the rumors she just heard from Montrell. "How could this be happening to me all over again?! And out of all people her! I kept her secret for many years!" Angie walked around in circles until it hit her. She picked up her cell phone and texted him. "CALL ME ASAP!" She then hung up and called the girl that he was supposed to have slept with. Again she got no answer. Angie plopped down on her couch, placed her head in her hands and cried. Revenge had sat in. She wanted them both out of her life for good.

Angie thought back to the very first time it happen to her, and how she allowed her lover to get away with cheating on her. Never again she promised herself after that Day of Atonement.

"It didn't work then, and it damn sho' ain't gonna work now!"

She got up ran into her room, went into her closet and found her Glock nine. Somebody was going to pay. As she check the clip to make sure she had bullets her phone rang, with haste she ran back into the kitchen and looked at the I.D. that read: 'BOBO My Husband'.

"Husband my ass; he's gonna be a dead husband when I get finish with him." she answered, "Hello."

"What's up baby?"

"I need for you to come home." Angie said calmly. "I need you now."

"I'm pulling up now."Just like that Angie hung up, cocked her nine and sat down on the couch. She looked at Moneeka's book on the coffee table only to add fuel to the fire. At that moment she heard a knock at the door. BOOM, BOOM, BOOM.

B'Shone

CHAPTER 20 Confession

"Doctor, tell me. How does it look for my son?" Keke asked, as she stood next to the Doctor as he examined Lil Dillin.

He shrugged his shoulders changing Dillin's I.V. "As of right now, it's hard to say. However, as long as he is stable, he has a good chance. With the technology we have today, I'm confident that he'll pull through."

Keke looked the doctor in his eyes. That's when she sensed a hesitation in his voice.

"I'll be here all night. Go home and get some rest. And if anything changes, good or bad, I'll personally give you a call."

"No, no, no." Keke said sternly as tears flowed down her face. "I can't leave my son by himself. He's all I got."

The Doctor walked over to her and gave her a handkerchief. He felt the pain that she was enduring. He had seen mother's like her come in time and time again with sons that want to live the street life but not knowing the consequences that comes along with it.

"Look, seeing your son like this is not good for you. You need to remember how he was before this. Just go home and I promise you I'll call you if there are any changes."

Keke walked over to her son's bed, kissed him on the forehead, and quickly turned and walked away. She knew if she would have stayed any longer she wouldn't have left.

The doctor restricted Lil Dillin visits for the next 48 hours, unless it was his mother.

***

"Come in!" Angie screamed as she stood in front of her front door with her pistol drawn ready to put two hot ones in BOBO. As her door swung open her visitors jumped to the side.

"Angie!" Moneeka screamed out. "What the fuck wrong with you?" She peeped back into the living room seeing Angie lowering her pistol. "Oh my gosh, Angie. I don't know what has gotten into you lately."

"Sorry, ya'll at the wrong place at the wrong time. I thought ya'll was, BoBo. I'ma blow his ass off the moment he walk through that damn door." Angie stressed as she pranced around in circles, then placed her gun on the coffee table.

Angie really didn't want Moneeka over her house right now. She looked at her and rolled her eyes. King noticed the tension. He then nodded for Big Runn to get the pistol off the table. The moment he did, King ups his pistol and aimed it at Angie.

"Where is that nigga of your?" King asked firmly. Angie couldn't believe that the director had a pistol to her head. She was baffled. A smile graced her face.

"I knew you was a gansta' ass nigga. Damn, why couldn't I get you befo' that hoe?"

"Angie!" Moneeka cried out. "I can't believe you would say that."

"Believe it bitch!" Angie had never called Moneeka out of her name. Needless to say, she was still upset from the last book signing. Angie looked to Big Runn, "you cute too, what's ya' name, Big Man?" Big Runn smiled, she was his type of girl; straight Hood.

King walked closer to her, "Now I'ma ask you one last time. Where is ya' nigga?"

"All my bad gansta." Angie smiled, putting up her hands as to be making kitty claws at him, and purred, "Purrr," she winked. "He should be bringing his punk ass through that door any minute now. I hope ya'll kill his bitch ass! Because if ya' not, ya'll might want to leave, cuz I'm killing his ass. He'll never cheat on me again with that nasty ass thang!"

The sound of keys sliding in the door caught all of their attention. Click and her door slowly came open. BoBo walked in with his head down as he dropped his bags off at the front door. He called out Angie name.

"Angie!" the moment he raised his head up Big Runn shoved his 45 into BoBo's mouth breaking a few of his teeth causing blood to spew out of his mouth. BoBo was caught off guard. With blood running and his hands held high he didn't know what to think. He looked over at Angie mean mugging him. Why? He didn't know.

A muffled sound came out of his mouth, "Baby." BoBo mouthed.

"Don't baby me now nigga!" Angie spit. "You wasn't sayin' baby when you was with that nasty ass thang!" Moneeka pulled Angie back down to the couch.

Moneeka whispered to her, "This is serious. I advise you to stop playing."

King walked over to BoBo, stood in front of him and stared directly into his eyes. Runn removed the pistol out of BoBo's mouth but placed the barrel to his temple.

"Who shot up the 1300 block of, Hyde Park?" As BoBo prepared to speak, King raised his index finger to his lips, "Now before you answer me, just remember this, I'm not going to ask you twice. If I even think that you're lying," King looked at Big Runn, "Off with his head. Now, who did it, and why were you there?" King glanced in the direction of Moneeka and said, "Get him some water."

"It was an accident. St. Louis Black, had beef with, Malcolm. Him, Scooter the Barber and Trickey were aiming to kill Malcolm's crew. But somehow things went wrong." Moneeka gave him the water and he took a sip. "I can't tell you what went wrong, because I didn't get out the car. I was instructed to stay in the car, and to be ready to drive off."

"Why?" King asked. At that moment King's phone rang. "Hello." He listened, "Stay with him. Call me later."

138

"I ain't ah killer. I was in Black's debt so he told me if I drove for him while he was in Memphis that my debt would be cleared."

"So, when they got back in the car, did they say who killed my nephew?" King asked.

"It was Trickey. But Trickey's dead. Someone from, Malcolm's crew, or your nephew's crew killed him in the shoot out."

King contemplated if he should kill BoBo or not. He knew if he did he stood a chance on either, Angie or Moneeka snitching on him, or better yet he would have to kill them both.

"Where's Black?"

"He took off to St. Louis, taking Scooter with him." BoBo lowered his head, "Leaving me here to die." Tears rolled down his face. He had heard of King's reputation, but never thought in a million years that he would feel his wrath.

"Kill his ass! He slept with that." Angie shouted.

"Angie, shut up!" Moneeka screamed.

"He shouldn't have cheated!" Angie barked back.

"You drove the get-a-way car that got my nephew laid up in the fuckin' hospital fighting for his fuckin' life!" King had gotten agitated. "So it's only right that you go visit him."

"I will, I will. I promise I will." BoBo cried.

POW...POW...POW, "I know you will." Big Runn put three hot

139

ones in BoBo. One in each knee cap, and one in his right shoulder, "now when you visit him, make sure you let him know that his uncle made you come visit, and you was the one driving the get-a-way car."

"Ahh! Ahh!" BoBo screamed as he laid on the floor.

"Call 911, and tell 'em that someone broke in on you and ya' man." King instructed Angie.

"Okay, if you let me put one in his bitch ass." Angie walked over to BoBo and commenced to kicking him in his legs, as he screamed out loudly. Moneeka grabbed her again pulling her down to the couch, "get ya' damn hands off of me!" She hated BoBo, and Moneeka wasn't too far down the list.

King leaned over to BoBo, "I'm going to let you live. But if this ever come up about what just happen. I'ma find you and put three in the back of your head my damn self. I'ma make you look like a fuckin' bowling ball, by the back of your head. Understood?" BoBo nodded yes, in agony.

Angie walked over to Big Runn rubbing his arm, "Can I just let him die right here?" Runn shook his head no, as he slapped her on the ass. "Ohhh...weee, Big Daddy, Angie likes it rough." She said picking up the phone dialing 911.

King looked over at Moneeka sitting in the far right corner of the couch scared for her life. She had never witness anything like this before, she was frighten. King knew he couldn't leave her with the state of mind she was in. The fear that raced across her face told the story. She'll tell. He walked over to her, kissed her forehead, and whispered "let's go baby." Took her by the hand and headed for the door. He looked back at Angie and winked, "Handle that." He passed her his number, "call me when it's done." She took that as a flirt, and winked back smiling.

B'Shone

CHAPTER 21 Dead Body

"Look, I'ma head over to the 13 and clear out the rest of that and have a couple of fiends board the trap back up for good." Big O said to Carmichael, while cleaning himself up. He knew sitting around feeling sorry for himself, and what happen to Lil Dillin wasn't going to solve anything. O knew in his mind that the only way to make things right was to kill the responsible party.

***

8:30 that night Big O drove down the 1300 block of Hyde Park and noticed that the street was quiet. Not too many fiends roaming the block and maybe a small-time dealer or two were out. He drove Carmichael's Honda Civic and went un-noticed.

He pulled into the drive way and drove straight to the back yard making sure no-one came knocking at the door because they saw a car in the yard. O reached over the back seat and grabbed his Victor's Secret duffle bags, checked his Glock, making sure it was loaded, and crept into the trap. Heading straight for the dope, he loaded it in a black trash bag, and the money in the two large duffle bags. He stood in the window looking down the block and thought about all the money he made in the 13. He was known as the real King. That life he couldn't let go of. Needless to say, it was about to come to an end. At that moment. O was thrown off track when he heard, BOOM! The back door came crashing down off its hinges.

"Get down, get down, get down don't you move!"Before O had a chance to react, he had a twelve gage aimed directly at his face.

"If you even think about it Big Boy, you'll have more holes in you than a pin cushion." That's when it hit him. He was being robbed. There he stood, the 6'2, 260 pound beast of a man. Snake! Everyone knew of his reputation, but he never tried to rob King's crew. King had pumped the fear of god in the streets back in his days, but now some didn't care, and Snake was one of them.

As O got ready to speak he heard a familiar voice coming from the back room. "Didn't I tell you that I was gonna get you? Didn't I tell you that you weren't gonna do what you wanna do and live to brag about it?"

O squinted his eyes trying to get a closer look at the voice coming out of the darkness. He wished that he would have turned the light on in the trap house now. However, as the voice entered the room, he was stunned. His eyes widened as he damn near had a heart attack.

Snake smiled, "Don't look so surprised, Big Boy, you looked as if you seen a ghost." Again he laughed as the voice came closer to him, "By the way, Lil Paul told me to tell you ain't shit personal, it's all business."

Snake looked down at the dope and money and decided to take it. "So I'ma take all of this." Slowly Shake leaned over and got the duffle bags and signal for the voice to get the dope.

"Lil Paul, also told me to tell you now it's over. Now you can get out the game, after you pay him his money that I'm taking. So I don't know what you're gonna do." Snake turned to walk out but spent around and said, "Now the game is over." He cocked the twelve gage and prepared to shoot O in the face, "Good night." Snake said.

BOOM! BOOM! His body hit the floor, and blood flew everywhere, as brain matter spattered against the walls. At that moment Cool-Aid and Ken entered the living room. Snake's girlfriend stood there and pissed on herself. Big O didn't know what to think. He was just blessed to be alive. O looked at the badge around Cool-Aid's neck and knew his reign was now over.

"You good, Big Boy. I've been friends with your brother for years. He called me the day he left town and told me to keep my eye on you. So when everything hit the fan I called him, before you took Lil Dillin to the hospital." Cool-Aid explained as he stood over Snake's body. "He knew all about you going to Nashville hooking back up with ex-wifey, and Lil Paul. The Feds knew that Paul was trying to expand his empire in order to get himself off his indictment." O lowered his head in disgust.

FLASHBACK

"A'ight, O. Be careful. Shit ain't the same as it was when you was running back and forth from Nashville to Memphis. Everybody is a snitch."

PRESENT

"That's what Nekka was trying to tell me. Fuck! How could I be so stupid?" O cried out.

Cool-Aid looked up at Big O, "You was gonna be his fall guy. That's why he kept sending you more work each time."

O was shocked to know that Cool-Aid knew how much work he was getting. "How you know what he was sending me?" O asked.

"Your brother knew. The truck driver that delivered that dope to you used to be a federal agent until he got fired for snorting drugs. Then he started working for your brother out of town and your brother took good care of him. He still had his connection with the Feds, so every time your name or his came up he would contact your brother."

O looked at Ken, "So I guess you a cop too?"

"Hell naw! I'm a muthafuckin* Pimp, and ah hustler! But once I found out that you were gettin' work from Paul. I called Tot. You do know Tot? Old school cat that keeps a toothpick in his mouth and Lite Bread in Nashville." O nodded yes. "They knew you were a pussy hound, and that you loved the game. So they told me to join your crew and to look out for you. Tot and Lite Bread, back in the day, gave your brother work. And they loved him. Why you think they never fucked with you?"

O was speechless. He was at a loss for words. He knew all of this came by greed. The number one cause of sending black men and women to prison or the grave.

"If you would have just listened to your brother, none of this shit would have taken place. That nigga loves you. If he didn't, Paul would still be alive and rotting in jail. But those niggas, Tot and Lite Bread,

146

well let's say this, you don't owe Paul shit." Ken explained as he turned to Recca. "And fo' you"

"I'll take care of this one." O cocked his hammer back. "Bitch you crossed me twice already, I promise you it won't be a third time. "

"O, please!" Recca begged for her life. Ex-wifey began to cry. "Paul told me to ride with Snake just to make you jealous. He said that he was gonna give me Ten racks. You know I needed that money." She cried. "O please don't kill me! Please!"

O reached into the bag and gave her ten racks. "Here catch."

Recca caught the money with trembling hands. She was shocked she thought that her life was over.

"Now what? What you're standing there for?" O asked her.

As she turned to walk out, she heard the first shot, POP. But not the next four.

POP, POP, POP, POP. O unloaded five slugs to her head and then walked over to her dead body, and got his money. "Bitch you'll never be able to spend it! I'll never strike out!"

O turned to Cool-Aid, "So how are we gonna handle this?" he pointed to the bodies on the floor. At that same time, in walked King, Moneeka, Big Runn, and his cleanup crew.

"You've fucked up enough. I'll handle it from here." King said and then turned to Cool-Aid. "Thanks for the call. If not his ass would be dead."

King signaled for his cleanup crew to dispose of the bodies. As the men picked up Snake's body, Moneeka got a closer look at his face she grasped for air, and stumbled back bumping into King.

"You okay? I told you to stay in the car."

A single tear trickled down her face. "That's... Snake."

Everyone attention quickly shifted toward her.

"And you know him, how?" King asked.

"He's the one that broke my heart." Moneeka admitted.

"Now you're crying over this nigga! Get this bitch outta here!" Ken stated.

"NO!" Moneeka shouted. For the first time in many years, she started talking like a black woman, as if she had some soul. She walked up on Ken and looked him in his eyes, and sternly stated, "I got ya' bitch between my fuckin legs!" she said grabbing her crotch. "And this one mutha fuckin' tear you see," she wiped her face, "Or seen. It was a tear of joy! Fuck him and you!" She quickly turned and noticed that Big O had laid his pistol down to help pick up the bodies. She snatched it off the table and fired two shots into Snake's dead body. The cleanup crew instantly dropped the body to the floor. Looked at her as if she had lost her damn mind.

"Now I'm to blame just as much as any of you in this house!"

King had placed a surprising smirk on his face. Another good girl gone bad he thought to himself. Or maybe he brought the dark side that was in her out.

"Let's go." King said.

***

Police was surrounding Malcolm's home preparing to serve a warrant. That's when they noticed all the windows on the front side of the house were busted, bullet holes through out, and the wooden front doors broken and open. Captain Lee Johnson signaled for a few officers to go around back.

As he prepared to go through the front he whispered to another officer "Take the right, and I'll take the left." They entered the house and noticed broken glass everywhere. T.V. turned over on the floor, and the house looked to be vacant, pictures dangling on the walls, and a radio remained on.

"Clear!" Captain Johnson yelled out.

"All clear in the back!" Another officer said coming up from the rear. "It seems to me that someone wanted him more than I did. Search the premises for a body, drugs, or anything else we can tie him to."

The MPD searched the house high and low and still came up empty handed. Unbeknownst to them, Malcolm was in the home in his secret hiding place watching them on surveillance. Malcolm's heart hit the floor after he seen Cool- Aid take off his mask revealing his identity on the monitor.

Taking a sniff of coke, Malcolm said, "I should have known that fat ass nigga was a cop!" he continued to look at them vandalizing his home.

He was glad that he didn't get it remodeled after Black shot it up.

"I'm glad K.P., is dead. Because if he wasn't, I would have killed him myself for bringing a narc to my spot. He's the reason they're in here now!" Malcolm knew it was time for him to leave just in case they find him.

"Pack'em up boys!" Captain Johnson shouted to his officers. "Officer Moore, I want you to get back to the station and put out an APB, on everybody that we have who are apart of Malcolm's, crew."

"What about, King's crew?" Officer Moore asked.

"I'll handle him myself." The Captain said, with a devilish grin.

***

"This just came down from a chick I fuck with who work for the Feds." Cool Aid said talking to King, as they sat inside the Holiday Inn Select lobby on Airways and Democrat. "She said that they got, Big O, on a Federal Indictment." King closed his eyes and lowered his head. He couldn't believe that it was happening again.

"WHY, WHY, WHY, WHY, WHY? That boy never had to sell dope!" King said taking a sip of his liquor. King couldn't understand for the life of him what was it that his brother loved so much about the street life?

"Did she say what proof they got?"

"Well from what she was able to gather. Apparently, O was

fucking with this Brazilian chick named El'vita who was DEA. When he sent her away with the driver to Vegas, the driver spilled his guts to her one night while they were getting high. But the good part about it, the driver got her on video getting high also." A slight smiled appeared on King's face. "Now don't get your hopes up high. The Feds, could easily said they knew that she was getting high not to blow her cover."

"What?"

"So we might can somehow get that evidence dismissed." Cool-Aid said, "But here's the crazy part. Before Lil Paul came up dead they had his phone tapped. They got all his people in Cali, St. Louis, Carolina, Nashville, and of course your brother."

"Fuck!" King grimaced threw his teeth. He was not trying to make a big scene, being that he was sitting in a public place.

Cool-Aid looked up side King's head and softly told him, "They wanted Lil Dillin also, but she told them that she didn't fell that he was gonna make it. And then she destroyed his film. However, she couldn't do it for O, because his name was ringing too much in Memphis."

"I owe you big time." King sipped on his drink and ordered them another round. He glanced over his left shoulder at Moneeka who was trying to sit at a table by herself watching T.V., but couldn't due to the unwanted attention she was getting from the airplane pilots that was coming into the lobby looking for someone to entertain them until take off time.

King knew that he couldn't baby sit her for the rest of his life, for her knowing that Big Runn shot BoBo, but whatever it took for her to get pass it, he would do for right now. Plus having her around had it perks.

King had gotten a call from Angie telling him that BoBo moved back to Richmond VA., and that he didn't talk to the cops. Big Runn put him in a wheel chair due to both of his knees were badly battered. BoBo didn't want any more trouble. He wasn't a gansta he was more of a player that got caught in a bad situation. King looked back at Cool-Aid.

"I'ma kill, St. Louis Black, you know that right."

"Yeah, but our main focus is to get your brother to turn himself in so it won't look so bad on him." King agreed. He knew that he had the best lawyers money could buy, and they had a good chance of beating those charges.

"But we have to get Scotter and Black first. He's not gonna do a day until he get the responsible party. I know him. He is hurting for what happened to Dillin. He'll kill himself if, our nephew dies while he in prison and didn't kill them. I don't think so."

"I gotta get outta of here; I'll holla at 'cha later." Cool-Aid said as he stood to walk out.

"I know your, Captain, still wants us. So he gots to go, too." They both nodded.

***

King escorted Moneeka up to the room that he got for them. He needed to clear his head. He took his shirt off, laid across the bed, and closed his eyes. He was exhausted. Moments later he drifted off into a deep sleep. He tossed and turned, as low moans crept from his mouth. He was having a bad nightmare. He woke up thirty minutes later in a cold sweat screaming, "NOOOO!"

Moneeka lying beside him woke up also, "Baby, what's wrong?" she asked as she got out of the bed and rushed into the bathroom and got a cold towel and placed it on his forehead. "You were just having a bad dream." She went on to wipe his chest.

Moneeka got out of the bed and took King's shoes off and then his pants.

He laid back and closed his eyes again only to open them to the moistness of her mouth going up and down on his shaft.

"Mummm." he moaned.

She stepped out of her clothes and slid down on him nice and slow.

B'Shone

CHAPTER 22 Trapped

Captain Johnson paced in his office, late Friday night, upset and mad about Malcolm and King not being behind bars. He decided to head out to his favorite drinking spot- Wing City.

As he headed towards Wing City, he drove up Airways Blvd, looking for some action before getting his freak on. He wanted to be in his right frame of mind if he was going to get his dick sucked. He wanted to be sure that it was her performance and not the whiskey. Unable to find someone, he turned into the parking lot, took off his blazer and tie, then headed for the door. As he entered, he walked straight for the bar.

"Vodka on the rocks, please." Captain said to the bartender, "Make that a double." He sat at the bar for about an hour enjoying the sound of Maze, and Frankie Beverly, 'JOY &PAIN'. He sang along with the rest of the party goers. He was feelings great. He had taken his mind off work for that moment; however, he never noticed that there were a set of preying eyes looking upon him the entire night..

Slowly, the hazel set of eyes stood and strolled over toward him sashaying her curvy hips with every step she took. The caramel skin tone bomb shell had hypnotized the Captain with those big pretty legs in her too short mini skirt. She stood in front of him not saying a word.

He couldn't take his eyes off of her firm perky breast and she knew it.

She inhaled just to make them stand up even more. He finally looked her in the face only to see her long tongue graze her lips and then touch her chin. Instantly he got an erection.

"Care to buy a lady a drink?" The young tender asked.

He smiled, "Sure. What you're having?" He asked, rubbing her hand as she sat down on the stool next to him, spreading her legs wide open to show him her pretty pink vagina. The Captain took his right hand and rubbed her neatly shaved legs feeling the smoothness of them, and again his erection showed through his grey slacks. "I want a Dick Gregory."

The bartender sat her drink in front of her, but before she took a sip she stuck her finger in it, twirled her drink around in circles and inserted that same finger in her mouth, then in her moistness.

The young tender took him by the hand and led him down stairs. "Let's go down stairs, it's much quieter." She cooed.

"Is anyone else down here?"

"No. We're gonna be alone." she said, squeezing his ass. They entered the private room, and she closed the door behind her. Little did the Captain know he was hypnotized by a whore that did any and every thing for money. He was bound to pay for her services, one way or another.

She led him over to a couch that was stationed in the far right corner of the room, which was dimly lit. She took his drink and placed it on the table, stood and danced for him seductively.

"You like what you see?" she asked, as she twirled around in front of him bending over touching her toes, as he witness that she had on no panties.

He reached down on the table got his vodka and took a big gulp, and loudly spoke, "I'm ready baby! Come to pappa!"

Slowly she made her way over to him, taking off her halter top letting it hit the floor. She straddled his lap as he buried his face in her breast. The young tender leaned back and got his drink, and gave it to him. "Here daddy."

Taking another gulp he was feeling right but woozy at the same time. Quickly she took his shirt off and dropped it to the floor, then unbuttoned his pants. She got down on her knees and pulled his little white penis out. With her majestic touch he was on cloud nine as she massaged his penis. She teased him nicely. Little did he know she had dropped a molly in his drink the first time she placed it on the table. He couldn't tell if it was her touch or the drugs.

His eyes slowly began to close as he kept a friendly smile on his face. "Here's ya' drink, daddy." The tender cooed after she squeezed three drips of eye drops in what remained of his drink.

After finding his eyes could barely stay open, she went into his pocket, got his wallet and took his money. "Two hundred dollars," she looked at him in disgust, "Broke ass cracka."

At that moment Bob Winbush (Mr. Information) entered the room.

He noticed how drowsy the Captain was. He looked at the young tender strangely. "What are you doing?" Winbush screamed. "That's enough, Ivy!" He said walking towards her. "Ya fuckin' name should be Posion Ivy, instead of, Sue Ivy. You one treacherous, BITCH!"

"I never leave my customer dissatisfied." she looked up at him, "And for ten racks, I'll drug you." She didn't blink her eye not once as she stared at him. He knew she meant business.

Sue Ivy had gotten inducted into the hustle game at the young age of 15. After her parents died in a plane crash, she found that she had no one to protect her. She learned how to fight, steal clothes, and make her own money. However, when she found out what her pussy was worth, and incorporated it with her killing skills, every pimp and hustler tried to get her on their team. Now 26-years-old, and still with that same innocent baby face, but full grown woman body she became the center of attention. Everybody wanted her.

"You can leave now, Ivy." Winbush told her as she put her BEBE halter top back on.

She patted his ass as she walked past him. Then, as she headed up the stairs, down came three men. One passed her a stack of money as the other one placed a blade in her hand.

Winbush took a bucket of ice water and dashed it in Captain Johnson's face. He quickly realized that he was tied to a chair.

Winbush sat him up in the chair the moment he found him unconscious. Fear sat in the Captain's heart. Spitting water out of his mouth and blinking his eyes to focus, he noticed the men standing in front of him. It was King, Big Runn, and Big O.

"You two!" Captain Johnson shouted. "Do you know who the fuck I am?" he said as he wiggled in his seat. "I'll have your asses for this, King!"

He hated the brothers with everything in him. "I should have killed you two the day I had a chance to." Again he squirmed, still tied to the chair. "That's okay! The lil half dead, sumbitch nephew won't live!" He shouted. "I should have told Black to kill his mammy first."

SLAP, PUNCH, KICKS combinations came from the three. Just the thought of Dillin lying in the hospital was enough to make Big O go crazy. Winbush had to restrain O.

"Come on, come on. He'll get his."

The Captain spit up blood as he coughed. Still high off the drugs, he really didn't feel that quick beating. "Y'all destroyed my family. Fat Azz and ya' nephew turned my two daughters into whores, sluts, dick sucking freaks!" Tears ran down his face, then he snarled at King, "And you! You ain't no fucking movie producer. You filmed my beautiful wife getting fucked in every hole on her body. I became the laughing stock on the job. Everybody's seen all her god given assets because of you! Now she in high demand. Everybody wants her!" He broke down and cried. "I loved my wife and kids, now I have nothing."

King's mind went totally blank after he heard the Captain say, "I should have told Black to kill his mammy first." He didn't hear anything else.

"So it wasn't an accident. You told Black to kill my nephew?" King asked.

"I told him to kill him and everybody else on the 13. Then the block would be his. He wanted the block, and I promised him that he could have it if he got rid of everybody else. Fuck you nigga! Y'all destroyed my…"

Before he could get the words out of his mouth, King damn near kicked his head off his body.

"Ahhhh!" The Captain screamed as he spit out a few teeth.

Winbush once again sat him back up right.

King stepped directly in front of the Captain and kneeled down where they could be eye level, "You tried to kill my family." He was livid.

Big Runn seen it in his man's eyes and slapped the fire out of the Captain with his pistol; blood went flying across the room. "Now I'm gonna film your wife and daughters fucking each other and sucking my dick. Then I'm piss in a cup and make each one of them take turns drinking it and calling me daddy while you watch." King stood and turned to walk away, "You ah lucky man. I ain't gonna kill you."

They all turned and left.

The Captain sat in the basement and screamed, but no-one could hear him due to the loud music. Unbeknownst to him, there was another entrance behind him. He panicked when he heard the sound of a door opening and closed. He slightly turned his head but couldn't see behind him. The clacking sound of shoes on the floor made him nervous.

"Who's there?" he screamed, "Show yourself!" The stranger walked up behind him and touched his shoulder. He jumped. "What do you want? You have to let me go. He said he wasn't gonna kill me."

"You asked what I want? I want ya' soul." At that moment a blade was placed to his neck. "And he didn't lie. He's not gonna kill you, I am." He got cut from ear to ear. The killer walked in front of him buck naked and danced. "This is what you want? Right daddy?" Ivy said.

Winbush walked back into the basement and stared at her. He shook his head. "You're one sick, Bitch!" as she continue to dance and licked her tongue out touching her chin with it. "Put ya' clothes on and get out of here." He was a little frightened of Ivy himself. She was a stone killer. Winbush knew not to allow his wife, Jackie, around Ivy. She would definitely turn her out.

Again, she got her clothes walked passed him, and patted his ass.

B'Shone

CHAPTER 23 Da Fire

"Let's get the fuck up outta this town." Malcolm told one of his soldiers as they prepared to vacate the city un-noticed. Although he hasn't been served by the FEDS, he knew that they were out to get him. And, with that knowledge, he had the heads up on them. Before he'd spend a day in prison, he'd be a fugitive on the run; doing time was not part of his future.

"Bring the car around back."

Malcolm peeped out the back door and jumped into his new Lexus he just bought last week in one of his cousin's name, his cousin had a great job, and he was a square; never been in any trouble, just what he needed.

Trailing close behind him was the rest of his crew. They also knew that they would be arrested if they stayed in Memphis. Malcolm laid his head back on the headrest as his man drove. He reminisced on the day he took over the 1300 block after King gave the game up. With a low tone he said, "Those were the days."

As his man continued to drive he thought about how him and Kelly P, used to walk in Pure Passion strip club and toss thousands of dollars in the air, and all the girls would flock to them, like the true players they were. To how his man Kelly P would always stutter and say something stupid, like "A...ah...ah... the gi..girl booty smmmmmmell good as hell."

"Hump, that was my dawg."

He continued to think about his dead homie until he remembered that Kelly P. is the reason he's on the run. 'That nigga served the narcs.' He thought to himself. "Damn, my nigga gone." He mouthed, but nothing came out. Malcolm even thought about all the freaks that would come around the trap and do any and everything strange for some change.

"Work it girl." he said softly smiling. He remembered Kita Red coming to the trap and doing his entire crew for two hundred dollars and four 20 packs of powder. Freaky, blow-head bitch." Those were the day when the streets where his.

With his eyes still closed, Malcolm twitched and squirmed in his seat. Bad memories invaded his thoughts. Ever since Big O came back to the 1300 block, things went sour for him. From O telling him that he was back on the block to stay, to him saying Malcolm was too small-time to serve his people, or bad mouthing him, in front of his crew, that he could buy from him, to him snorting coke; it was all bad.

Malcolm had gotten so wrapped up in being the man that he lost track of what the game was all about. Simply make enough money then get out. Big O had took so much of his business that he started snorting more and more each day, which caused him to start coming up short on St. Louis Black's money.

"Muthafuck!" Malcolm shouted, as his eyes opened. "I lost 90% of my customers because of his fat ass!" The redness in his eyes was clearly showing.

"Turn this car around and go by the 13." He told his driver.

"Mai, it's 9:00. With-in the next hour the police will be changing shift and that night shift crew hates us. You know damn well that they will be out to get us." his driver said.

"Fuck'em!" he screamed. "Go by the 13!"

"You're the boss."

"Damn right I am!" he was pissed. He thought about how Black sprayed his mansion and his cars to him having to vacate his own home. To the shoot out that ended with Kelly P. coming up dead.

***

As they turned on the 13, Malcolm quickly jumped out of the car and rushed into his old trap house and went to the back and got a can of gasoline. He made ten Molotov cocktails.

"Here." he said to his crew giving each one of them one. "Hit Big O's trap house, the duplex next to his, Aaron and Lil Allen James' trap, and Craige P's spot. Burn'em all down!"

As instructed, with-in five minutes the 13 was going up in flames. Malcolm and crew loaded up to leave until he seen a fiend that knew him well.

"Come here, Critter." He called the short no teeth white boy over to him. "Let every hustler that works these streets know that Alabama 'Muthafuckin' Malcolm did this shit! Tell them niggas I said fuck'em all!" He tossed Critter his last personal snort pack as he got ready to drive off. However, quickly he jumped out his car and took the pack back from the fiend. "Here's twenty dollars, I need this shit." he hopped back in. "Now let's go. Alabama, here I come."

Malcolm's inside was burning. He wasn't going to leave well enough along. He wanted Big O and Black. Revenge had to eat.

"After the smoke clears, we're heading to St. Louis. Black is walking dead."

CHAPTER 24 Truth Revealed

"Say playa, the 13 is up in smoke." Ken explained to Big O over the phone.

"What you mean?" Big O asked.

"Just about every house on the block is on fire." Ken paused, "Matta fact, everybody's spot except Malcolm's."

"That black bitch!" O screamed.

He looked to the left of him at King who was driving them to his crib in South Wynn, and told him the bad news. O went on and assured him that there wasn't anything left in it. King could care less about what was in the house; it was the fact that it was his grandmother Laura Mae's house. Her and their grandfather spent their entire life in the house and to have it burned to the ground was something he was not willing to accept. King had just reached another level of anger for his brother. He said nothing.

"That fiend Critter told me that he seen Malcolm do it. And he bragged about it and said he was going back to Alabama," Ken said to O.

Malcolm felt that he was always safe when he was in his own city, however, King vowed to his grandfather and father that he would take good care of the house and Big O. Malcolm, along with St Louis Black was walking dead. Although King wasn't in the game, he was still well-connected.

O knew by the expression on King's face that he was fed up with him and everybody else in the city.

"Good looking out. Keep us informed." O hung up as he rested his head back on the headrest, and closed his eyes. For several minutes King said nothing until he couldn't take it any longer. While driving, he reached over and hit his brother in the jaw as hard as he could, then slammed on breaks bringing the car to a streaking halt.

"All this shit is your fault! Greedy! Just plain greedy!" King shouted.

By the time O gathered his self, and with the street mentality with in him, he reacted as such. Without thinking he reached for his pistol, as his thumb quickly grazed across the safety releasing it and pointing it at King's face. POW! The gun went off, and O lowered his head.

***

Angie sat in her living room drinking Ciroc and cranberry juice, as she read Moneeka's book. As she read, some chapters made her laugh, some made her cry, and some made her mad as hell. "Oh...that bitch!" she screamed out to herself, as she continued to read. "My girl is one freaky bitch!"

Two hours had passed and she was still reading. Nearing the last few chapters, Angies's eyes turned red. Her hands started to shake nervously, as her bottom lip began to quiver. "I knew it. How could she have known?" She paused, took a big gulp of Ciroc and started back reading. She was so upset that she didn't notice that she took a gulp of Ciroc straight out of the bottle.

Before she could finish reading the last chapter there was a knock at her door. She threw the book down on the table, stood up and yelled out. "Who the fuck is it?" she commenced walking towards the door.

Without looking through the peep hole to see who is at the door, she swung it open frowning. To her surprise, it was Tess. Another bitch on her shit list.

"Girl, what got your thong up your ass?" Tess asked as she walked in and took a seat.

Angie rolled her eyes and switched back over to her couch. Tess was unaware that Angie knew all about her and BoBo fucking.

Angie took another swig of her drink as she plopped down on the couch next to Tess and gawked at her. "I just finished reading this bitch's, book before I realized who she is."

"Girl, you're talking in circles." Tess said, fixing her a glass of Ciroc. Angie nodded yes. She wanted her to be intoxicated just in case she had to take flight on her. "What you talkin' bout?" Tess asked, as she kicked off her shoes.

Before Angie could open her mouth to say anything her phone rang and she jumped up and ran over to her kitchen counter to get her cell phone.

She looked at the caller I.D., 'Moneeka'.

"Speakin' of the devil, she will call." she answered with hostility. "What bitch!"

"Oh my gosh, Angie. What's wrong now?" Moneeka asked. "Never mind open the door."

At that moment Tess said, "Girl I'ma go take a nap." Again Angie rolled her eyes at her, as she walked toward the door, and snatched it open.

But there was no Moneeka. A few seconds later she came up the steps.

Moneeka entered the house not knowing what to expect out of her friend, but she knew something was wrong. Moneeka could tell by the look in her eyes.

As she entered, she looked around the room, "No bodies lying around" she thought to herself. Angie slammed the door behind her.

"I've finally read ya' book!" she shouted, looking Moneeka in the eyes.

"Did you like it?"

"How could you?"

Moneeka stood there puzzled, "Angie, what are you talking about?"

"The eyes. I was cool with everything in it until I read the part

170

where you said, and I quote," Angie rushed over to the couch and got the book and turned to the chapter, "I only knew of one person with those eyes. Mickie Peirson."

"Okay and...your point is?"

"Everybody Wants Her. Micole Peirson. Nobody wanted Mickie. We've been friends for ten years. I knew this was about your life. You one scandalous bitch. You'll do whatever you have to do, to keep your image intact. I knew it was you from the book signing in, New York. I wanted you to finish reading that chapter but you stopped! You knew I would figure it out then!" she cried.

"Angie, why are you crying?" Moneeka walked toward her with her arms open to embrace her friend, but only walked into a slap. "ANGIE!"

"I've had plastic surgery three times to keep my identity a secret."

Angie took her fake hazel contacts out of her eyes and threw them on the floor. "Look into my eyes, Bitch! I was fine the way I was until you posted my pictures all across face book, and tweeter!"

"Who? When did I do that? And why would I do that?"

"The gig is up, Micole!"

"Micole." Moneeka laughed, "You think I'm, Micole?" She quickly stopped laughing when she seen that Angie held a pistol in her hand.

"Now I have to start my life all ova again!" She aimed it at her

171

friend, "but you won't be alive to tell this story." POP! Moneeka cringed where she stood. Angie shot at the couch just to scar her. She had more conversation for her. Moneeka's hand flew over her mouth. "Now it's hittin' you."

"Angie, you're, Robin?"

"The one and only. See it didn't hit me the first time you said that you had surgery after your first novel, but when you talked about the eyes

I examined your eyes." Moneeka stood there trembling in her Prada pants suit.

"Angie, it's not what you think." Moneeka cried.

Angie's hand shook nervously, as she fired another shot at Moneeka's feet. Tears ran down her face profusely. She was confident that no one would ever know that she murdered her husband Shone, or at least never suspected it to be her, with all the surgeries she had. She knew she was in the clear. Now it was time to make Moneeka disappear.

"Please, Angie. I didn't know that you were, Robin, and I'm..."

"Shut up!" Angie screamed, "You ain't gonna get nobody else man!"

"Angie, that's why I talked about the scars on her ass and breast,." Moneeka dropped her pants and turned around so that Angie could see that she didn't have any scars on her ass. Her ass was naturally big."You couldn't have finished reading the book, because if you would have, you would have known, Micole was a man! Shone slept with a man!"

Angie titled her head slightly to the left thinking to herself, "Could this be true."

"I didn't know this was a true story. I received this story from a stranger, who mailed me everything that happened. She told me she wanted to be a writer, but wanted to know if it was good enough to publish. She said that if I wrote it verbatim and got it to go number one, she would then know she had what it took to be a writer." She paused for a reaction but got none. "They never mentioned anything about killing Shone. Hell I didn't either." Moneeka pleaded for her life. "Please read the ending."

Angie paced her living room, with the gun in hand. Someone knew her secrets and she wasn't safe. She stood there contemplating if she should kill Moneeka or not, until Tess walked out of the back room.

As the living room light shined so brightly on Tess face, Moneeka squinted her eyes at her. These two had had run ins several time, but this was the first time that she had gotten a close up on her.

"Tess, you might wanna go back to the bedroom," Angie paused, "fuck it." she waved her gun at her, "Stand ya' no good ass ova there too."

"Girl, stop waving that damn gun. I heard all the commotion, so I came up here to see what's going on."

"Shut ya' dyking ass up. I thought you was my friend too, but ya stanky ass fucked my man also! He admitted it to me!"

173

Again Moneeka looked at Tess, as she eased her pants back up around her small waist. "Now I remember. It was you that drug and raped me when I was in college." Tess started to clap her hands.

"I thought that you would never figure it out." Tess smiled. "I couldn't have you back in the day, but in college you really enjoyed me."

She leaned over and licked Moneeka's face. Angie looked confused. "Stop acting as if you didn't want me." Tess cooed.

"You drugged me!" Moneeka screamed.

"From the first time I ate that sweet, hot, tight cunt that no-one on campus wanted you fell in love." Angie was still confused. "Then at ya' book signing. I saw you when you closed your eyes and came on yourself by watching me play with my pusssssy." Tess slapped Moneeka on the ass.

But not without getting punched in the face, that was a side of her that Angie had never seen. Tess' lips begun to bleed. She simply licked her lip, and blew Moneeka a kiss.

"Uummmm.... taste just like period juice. So sweet." Tess winked. "And let's not forget Club Flirt in the ladies' room. I asked you to join. You were speechless. You started playing with ya' breast until Angie walked in to get you." Tess looked at Angie, " That's why she was in a rush to get you outta there. If you would have waited just a few minutes longer I would have been eating that hot pussy."

Moneeka continued to look upside Tess's head, that's when it hit her, "It's you! It's you!" She shouted, "It had to be you. Why else

174

would you show up at every book signing I had? You wanted to make sure I read the book the exact way you wrote it!" Again Tess started clapping. Finally she had figured it out. It had been Tess all along. She had been sending Moneeka the story week after week. Angie was now fumigating.

"It was you? How did you know my life unless" Angie walked closer to Tess and stared at her eyes. "Micole Peirson. Or should I call you, Mickie?"

"You two are so dumb. Mickie was my twin brother. I'm his sister Vickie. "Tess twirled around in a circle nice and slow. She even dropped her pants and took off her shirt revealing no marks on her body. "No scars," then Tess dug into her vagina with her finger, and placed it to Moneeka's nose. "All woman. You smell that sweet pineapple scent?" she laughed. "But after my brother died, I promised him that I would get even with everyone that treated him like shit! Girls that talked about how ugly he was and the guys that use to pick on him. Mickie changed into Micole and started fucking with every guy that hated on him. And he had it all on camera. They all fell in love with his ass hole. And the head he once gave them. Now after he finished with them, I sent all of them a video of them having sex with Mickie and if they wanted their secret to stay a secret, they had to pay. So of course they all agreed to pay. And when they did pay, I sent them another letter letting them know that Mickie had aids."

Moneeka and Angie took a step back. They didn't know what to think, do, or say. All they knew was Mickie became Micole. Tess continued. "Now as far as the women go. I fucked them just to show them that they wasn't shit! They could have fucked with my brother."

Angie stood there crying. Just the thought of having aids, made her sick at her stomach. She aimed her pistol at Tess and fired one in the hip.

"Bitch, you ruined my life!" Angie cried, "I never did shit to you or your dead ass brother!"

Tess laid on the floor in agony, "You and Shone talked about my brother throughout high school." She squinted in pain. "So after his surgery he gave Shone the head job of his life. All he talked about was how good ya pussy was. But he fell in love with my brother's ass hole!"

"So you wanted to hurt me? Bitch, you one sick hoe!"

"No sicker than you when you killed Shone and buried him in the woods by Martin Luther King Park. Mickie seen it all. But died before he could report ya' no good ass!" Tess stressed in agony then smiled. "Bitch you need to get tested because you might be H.I.V. positive!"

POW, POW, POW, POW, POW, POW, Click...click...click.

"Die bitch die! You ruined my life!" She looked at Moneeka and aimed it at her although she was out of bullets; she pulled the trigger anyway.

"And you helped her!" Moneeka could have cared less. All she thought about was having HIV. Angie was in a trance. "I could have HIV." She dropped the pistol and fell to the floor. Angie crawled over to her phone to call King. She knew he would help her get rid of the body, since she didn't call the laws on him. Now she wished she would have killed BoBo. "He slept with Tess and she might have Aids

176

too." Angie thought to herself.

"Hello, let me speak to, King." Instantly she stopped crying. "King what? in the hospital. Where? The Med." Moneeka eyes widened when she heard King's name, and the fact that he was in the hospital. She knew it had something to do with his brother.

Angie stood to her feet and looked at Moneeka. "Help me get this nasty bitch in the bathtub until I can get her outta here.

B'Shone

CHAPTER 25 Lost Souls

Tears echoed throughout the hospital lobby and waiting room, as others stood off to the side holding on to the ones who needed comforting the most. The Doctor came out to render the bad news, as more screams filled the air.

Every worker that was once part of King's T.B.F squad all stood in attendance. There were so many people that the waiting room and hallways couldn't contain any more of the Hayes family and friends. It was so many people crying that a few R.N's stood around comforting the family, while other members huddled amongst themselves. Big Runn stood off to the side by the vending machine, mean mugging Big O. He knew that all of this commotion was caused by O's selfish ambition. Big O stood off to himself staring off into space. He looked as if he had lost his best friend. He too kept his distance from everyone.

Moments later, Angie and Moneeka looked around not knowing what to do or who to talk to, until Angie spotted Big Runn, by the vending machine, as she rushed over toward him, a few tears ran down his fat round face.

"Hey, Big Man. Do you member me?"

He looked and saw the two standing in front of him and nodded yes.

"How does it look?" Angie asked, as Runn shook his head no, closing his eyes at the same time.

He was speechless. Runn had no words for no-one at that moment.

Moneeka's heart fell in her stomach. It was easy to tell how saddened she was by the undaunting expression that was written across her face.

The way she leaned forward clutching her stomach and crying told the story.

"No...no...no...this can't be true. He's got to be alright." She spoke just above a whisper as she collapsed on the floor. Angie leaned over to help her up, but to no avail, Moneeka resisted her courtesy.

Big Runn lifted her off the floor and placed her on the couch. Quickly, Angie sat beside her to comfort her again.

Several family members looked on at her and whispered amongst themselves. "Which one is that? She had to be one of his freaks. He had plenty." An older woman softly stated.

"Or, maybe she truly loved him." another said. The Doctor came out again, with yet another disappointed look on his face. Silence filled the air.

***

"Tape this entire area off." the Forensic Specialist said to the

M.P.D. "I don't want any of you to touch a thing. Everything is considered evidence. I'm pretty damn sho' they made some kind of mistake." Again he looked around the area. "This body was dropped here. Look." He pointed, "A body this size would have left more blood than this. It's like there wasn't any blood drained from him."

They had received an anonymous call from a stranger telling them that there was a body behind the dumpster of Nite & Day corner store, at Chelsa and Springdale. The Specialist knew the area all too well. He was also aware that the store had been closed for nearly six months. However, the smell was too much for the elders in the community. Which they never told shit that happened in the Hyde Park area. But the odor was so strong that it reeked of death.

The face of the deceased was gravely disfigured. Unrecognizable. The Specialist noticed that the body had a wallet sticking out of it side, as if someone placed it there. He kneeled down and got it. 'Captain Johnson.' He read.

"Fuck! It's Captain Johnson. They can stop the search for him now." Everyone stood around speechless. He looked at how badly beaten he was, and the deep laceration across the Captain's throat, and knew that this was no accident. "Who ever did this took a blade to his throat, and brass knuckles to his face and head. I can tell by the groves in his forehead." He pointed to bruises.

A rookie detective asked, "Who would do something so malicious to him?"

The Specialist looked up at him and gave an indignant stare. He was one person that knew of Captain Lee Johnson evil ways. There

181

were several people he could have thought of that wanted him dead.

He also knew if the Captain had it in for you, he would travel to the ends of the earth to get his man. He would not be satisfied until his mission was accomplished. However, this time it back fired on him, and the Specialist wasn't in a hurry to seek justice for him. For all he cared, this case was closed.

"Who wouldn't?" he answered, "trying to find the killer would be like finding a needle in a haystack." At that moment the coroner pulled up to take the body away. "Pack'em up. Let's go." As he prepared to walk off, he noticed a small wallet-size picture blowing in the wind. Quickly he caught up with it and looked at the sexy female's portrait. "Who is this young beauty? And why is her picture back here?" He stood and looked around and seen no one in sight. Unbeknownst to him, there she stood watching everything. Posion Ivy.

***

"Tell us something." Big O walked up to the doctor, however, Keke rushed over to where he was standing and slapped the shit out of O's mouth. She was hurting all over again. She hadn't been the same since her son Dillin was shot.

"All this! All this shit!" she pointed to everyone in the lobby, and hallway crying. "All this shit is your fault! You just couldn't leave well enough alone. You just had to live that fucked up life!" Keke screamed.

"Now our family is crumbling in front of our eyes!"

The Doctor had heard enough. He stepped in between the two.

"Hey! Enough! This is a hospital! Not a boxing ring. If you two want to fight, you will have to take that outside." He pointed toward the door. "This is a time to come together in prayer, not in yelling and playing the blame game. " He paused and lowered his tone, "Now I know that he is well loved, but I will hate to have to get the authorities up here for you, in your time of hurt. But you all need to get it together. So I'ma ask everyone to leave."

"I'm not leaving my baby." Keke cried.

"Y'all heard what the man said. Let's get up outta here." The deep voice penetrated across the crowded lobby. Angie and Moneeka turned to leave, but stopped in their tracks. It was him. Moneeka's eyes widened as she ran into his arms.

"Oh my gosh, King." Moneeka said, wiping her nose and eyes from all the crying she had done the last hour. "I thought. Well, Angie said that you was in the hospital."

King looked confused.

As Angie looked up at Big Runn, who was now standing next to King, she explained "He said," Angie pointing at Runn, "That you was in the hospital."

Runn shook his head no, "I told you he was in the hospital, because I was outside parking the car. His phone fell out of his pocket as he jumped out of the car. Before I could tell you that they called the family to come to the hospital because they thought that Lil Dillin was about to die, you asked for a room number then hung up."

Moneeka stood there shaking him head. All that crying was for nothing. She held on to King for dear life. She whispered in his ear, "I thought something bad had happened to you."

King glanced over his shoulder at his brother. Something did happen but he would never tell her. King held a dark spot in his heart for Big O.

To pull a pistol on your family, and fired it in his sunroof was something that he never expected from his own brother. O had to pay for all the wrong and greedy acts he committed. His mistakes, and the fact that no-one wanted him around fueled his rage.

Big O seen it in King's eyes when he pulled the pistol on him; King wasn't afraid to die. O knew he made a grave mistake. He should have killed his brother. All he had now was the little money made while doing his dirt. He was committed to making things right. However, he was so stuck on himself, that he didn't know where to start.

"Let's go." King said, he turned and looked at Angie, "You called me for something. What's up?"

Angie walked up to him and whispered in his ear, "I have another dead body in my house."

King frowned and looked at Big Runn, "Get the cleanup crew, and take her with you."

Keke walked over to King, "Brother, I need you to please get some of those high dollar doctors to come and take care of my baby."

"Dillin, gonna be just fine. The high dollar doctor is, God, and he's not for sale. He wanted you to cry out to him." Keke was shocked to hear him talk like that. King had been a gansta all his life, and to hear him talk about God was something new to her. A sigh of relief came over her at once. She felt good. She turned and walked past Big O, and lowered her head in disgust. "I'm gonna get him if my son die." she said, to herself.

Before Angie walked off, she pulled Moneeka by the arm and whispered in her ear."I'm sorry about what happened. But I want you to go with me in the morning. I'ma go get checked. Please go with me."

"I will girl."

"I'ma stay at the Hilton, on Mill Branch and 240. Come pick me up from there." She paused as a tear trickled down her cheek. "I'm scared as hell. It just don't feel right. Why would she tell me I need to get tested? Unless she got it, right?" Angie asked.

"Listen, first thing first. Get the bitch body out of your house, before you be in jail, instead of the grave. Then we'll see about everything else in the morning. Like King, said. Cry out to, God."

B'Shone

CHAPTER 26 No Pain No Gain

King pulled up to his house in South Wynn, as his garage went up.

To come to this house, you had to be a special person of interest. Moneeka had to be the one. They exited his Benz, and entered his house through a door that led into the laundry room. As he turned his alarm off he told Moneeka to make herself at home.

This had been one long week for King. He was exhausted. He walked into his master bedroom and started his bathwater and turned the Jacuzzi jets on allowing the bubbles to form. He walked into the living room where Moneeka sat on the couch, lost in her train of thought.

"The kitchen is to the right if you want something to drink, and if you're hungry call, Pizza Hut, or Southern Blaze Hot Wings, they have delivered here before." He told her nonchalantly. He turned to walk back to his bathroom, but stopped. "Just leave your bags in the car. I'll get them after I relax for a minute."

King turned and walked into his private room and closed the door behind him, and scanned threw his surveillance making sure that no-one tried to tamper with his property. He knew with all the stupid shit his brother had gotten into within the last month, anything was possible. King knew that it was only a matter of time before the FEDS came knocking at his door.

Moneeka stood in the kitchen admiring the red marble counter top, and the deep dark stain cabinets. She opened the refrigerator and saw a bottle of Merlot Red Wine. Fixing herself a glass of wine, she too knew she needed to relax from all the stress, and disappointments she had to endure over this last month. She thought back to her book signing, getting raped in college, to shooting Snake, to finding out that she was writing about her best friend's life.

She pondered over if she bought this curse upon her life with the selfish deeds, and acts she had committed. Or was it just the luck of the draw. Whatever it was, she wasn't trying to visit that life again.

She walked around King's mansion taking in his exquisite taste. She loved the deep dark brown leather sofa that matched his brown hard wooden floors. Her eyes widened after she stepped down stairs into his movie room and noticed the biggest TV she had ever seen in her life. She thought her 75 inch was something, but King had a 150 inch television. She was truly impressed.

"Oh my gosh! This man has a TV that is only in China right now. And to think with my nasty attitude I almost missed out on having him in my life."

King's movie theater was like a franchise theater. There was a ticket booth, popcorn machine, a fully stocked bar area, vending machine, and ten arcade games. Don't forget the twenty-five reclining seats.

Slowly, Moneeka strolled back up the stairs as her hand glided along the glass spiral staircase. She peeped in every room, sipping on her wine until she stumbled across King relaxing in his Jacuzzi with his eyes closed. The water dripped from his bald head, as his chest heaved up and down. At that sight alone she was turned on. Moneeka contemplated if she wanted to go down that road again with him, and get in the water to soak.

"Yes I do." she mouthed, but nothing came out. Gently, and quietly she placed her glass of wine on the counter and quickly got out of her clothes, letting them hit the floor, as she prepared to get in the Jacuzzi, but not before getting her glass of wine. She knew if she was about to embark on another sex journey with him, she needed to have something in her hand to soothe her nerves. She ran back into the kitchen and got the entire bottle. She walked back into King's master bathroom, and took a gulp straight out the bottle, then filled her glass back up.

As she stepped into the large Jacuzzi, King never knew that she was there, she eased up on him. "Here," she handed him the wine, as he opened his eyes. "I felt that you might need this." she said as she got behind him massaging his broad shoulders, felling the tension. "I feel the tension in your shoulders. You're too tight. All this built up stress is not good for you, baby." She said, out of concern. King was really feeling her; however, he never revealed his true feelings to a woman until he knew that she is down with him.

He simply said, "I know."

Seductively, Moneeka asked, "Is there anything," she cooed, "that I can do for you?" she nibbled on his ear, "that would help release some of this tension." Again she nibbled on his ear. Little did Moneeka know King's mind was a thousand mile away from home. It didn't matter what she said, he wasn't paying her any attention until she started massaging his penis.

Quickly she bought him back from space. King's mind was on his nephew being shot, how he let his father down, his grandparents house burning down and his own brother pulling a pistol on him.

"King, do you hear me?" she asked as she continued to massage his now erect penis.

"Oooh...uumm...yeah." he moaned as she licked his neck.

Softly she asked, "So tell me baby. What is it that you would like for...me...to...do?"

"Well, this is always good." King finally opened his eyes.

Moneeka's flawless body rose up out of the water and stood in front of him as the water glistened off of her body. King admired every curve in her body. He always wanted to get to this point with her and now was the time. He reached up and pulled her back down to him, taking her nipple into his mouth, teasing it with his tongue.

"Uumm," she moaned, as she sat in his lap, with his hand squeezing her ass. She took her right hand, grabbed his large penis and guided it into her now warm wetness. "Ooh, King." she moaned as she bit down on her bottom lip. Flashback of the first time she got in the shower with him came rushing over her at once. This time it was more pleasurable.

Slowly, Moneeka went up and down on his shaft like a veteran jockey rider. Water splashed on the floor wetting their clothes.

As the sex heated up, the mirrors begun to fog, from the steam of the Jacuzzi and the hot sex. Moneeka leaned forward, placing her hands on the other side of the tub, with King behind her.

She screamed, "Get it baby! Ooh get it, baby! It feels so gooooood!"

With every cry he went faster. King stroked her from the back while slapping her on her rearend. He lay back as she climbed back on top of him. Within minutes King had both of her legs in the pit of his forearms. He stood up with her and walked her into his bedroom and laid her in the bed. He penned both of her thick brown thighs to the headboard, as he licked the inner back calf of her leg.

King stood up in her warmth and shoved everything he had into her tight vagina. Quickly Moneeka placed both of her hands to his hips stopping his powerful thrust. To no avail.

"Noooo!" she screamed out.

He wasn't intentionally trying to hurt her, but he was.

"King!" Moneeka screamed, "You're in my stomach!"

The anger he had for his brother had begun to come out all at once. He wanted to punish his brother for all the dumb shit he put him through over the last mouth. With that in mind, he took it out on her. He forcefully shoved everything he had in and out of her.

"Please stop! Please, King! Sto...sto...st...stop!" her breathe became choppie. Her words shorten.

"Shut up! Take it! You're always complaining!" he screamed at her.

"King, I'm Moneeka. Stop! I didn't say nothing, baby!" She struggled to get away. "Stop! Stop! Don't! Nooooo..."

It was too late. His penis slipped out of her vagina, and plopped directly into her rectum. King was so lost in his anger that he never knew, until he finally came and collapsed on top of her, snapping back to reality.

She cried like never before as she forcefully shoved him off of her. She balled up in a fetus position.

"What's wrong?" He gently asked.

Crying she softly mumbled, "King, you didn't have to...treat me like that."

He was at a loss for words.

She got up and ran herself a tub full of hot water, sat in it and cried. She wanted to pay King back for taking his frustration out on her but it was hard when you have found love again.

"I'm so sorry, Moneeka. Please forgive me."

CHAPTER 27 Trapped

"You ready to go?" Moneeka asked Angie in a depressing tone.

Her body ached from the sexual frustration she had to endure last night. Needless to say, King cuddled and comforted her the entire night. Moneeka had to be a pain freak, because later that night she wanted more. But that time King made passionate love to her. He was truly apologetic. Moneeka realized that King had been through a lot in his life. He opened up to her and told her his life story and explained that he meant her no harm.

"Why the long face? I should be the one looking like that." Angie stated.

Moneeka smiled, "Oh My Gosh. Ang, if you only knew. My ass hole is hurting like hell but in a crazy way, I want to try it again."

"You freaky, bitch!" Angie joked.

"King and I were making love until his fat ass dick plopped in my ass. Girl, let me tell you." Moneeka rambled on and on about last night, until she glanced over at her friend staring out of the window with a sadden expression that invaded her face. Angie continued to peer out the window as she wiped away her tears.

"Oh my gosh, Angie. I'm sorry. I didn't mean to talk about...I'm sorry. I for...got." Moneeka said as she lowered her tone.

Angie shook her head no, "It's not your fault. I'm happy that you got your grove back. Stella!" they laughed. Moneeka knew that her friend was terrified. "What if she did have aids? Would she kill herself? Would she try another relationship? Would she move away? Would she go after BoBo?' All these questions ran through Moneeka's mind.

"Even though it was painful, I'm glad for you." Angie said putting on her poker face. Something she was good at was making people think that everything was alright with her even when they weren't. She just wanted to disguise her heartache and pain.

Angie had always been a good hearted person. Never tried to take advantage of anyone and would give you her last. However, to be facing the possibility that she might be HIV positive was much more than she could bear. It had an overnight effect over her life. She wanted so badly to sleep with Big Runn, but couldn't fathom giving him an incurable disease. In a matter of minutes her fate would be decided. She didn't want the same for him.

Moments later, Moneeka turned on Jefferson Avenue and parked in front of Memphis Health Department. They both sat in the car without saying anything or getting out. Moneeka saw a tear roll down Angie's face and she took her hand.

"Ang, you're going to be alright." Moneeka stated as she gently rubbed her hand. "Let's pray." Moneeka suggested and they both closed their eyes. "Dear God, if it be your will, be with my friend

Angie as she goes in here to get her body checked. Lord, we all make mistakes, so please give her and me another chance to make it right. We need you to show up on her behalf. Please. She needs a clean bill of health. In Jesus' name we pray, Amen."

As they prepared to walk into the health department, they notice a young teen coming out with a pink form in her hand crying and talking to herself.

"This can't be right. I've only been with one person. How can I have HIV?" the teen cried as she sat down on the bench in front of the clinic.

"Oh my gosh, Moneeka. What if that be me in a matter of minutes?" Angie nervously asked.

"Just have faith." she suggested as they walked in.

***

King walked through his home packing up everything he was going to need for his trip. He picked up the phone and called Big Runn.

"Big Man, meet me at my spot down town. Bring ya' thangs. We heading to St. Louis. It's time." King walked into his walk-in closet and got his two twin colt 45. He hadn't picked them up in years. He loaded them and placed them into his brief case. Closing it, he softly stated, "It's been a long time since I've played with you two." King haven't killed or thought about killing no one in many years. He was living a great life up until a month ago. However, it was in him. He had to show Black that fucking with a member of the Hayes family meant death. Needless to say, he had to teach his brother a lesson. He refused to allow him to do all that crazy shit and nothing happen to him. He had to learn once and for all.

"Get ready. We heading to St. Louis. Meet us at the spot downtown." He told his brother.

Thirty minutes later the three of them was outside of King's spot loading up his Black on Black Yukon, preparing to go handle business.

"We going down there, do what needs to be done and come right back. No fucking partying; strictly business." He stressed that to his brother. "Kill who we came to kill and no one else." Runn stated looking directly at O.

O hadn't said a word from the moment he pulled up. He was feeling like an outcast. Like in a game of chess, sacrifice the pawn to get to the king, and he felt like the pawn. Before they all loaded up, King pulled O to the side. "Regardless of your ignorance, you're still my brother, and I love you no matter what happens." King kissed him on the cheek and got into the truck.

O didn't know how to take it, never the less, he got in the back seat.

They pulled out of his condo garage onto Front Street and made a right onto Poplar Avenue. Big Runn popped in the Krunk City New cd, as they jumped on 1-55 North heading for St. Louis.

Unbeknownst to the three of them, an undercover vehicle was trailing them. Just as they made it across the Mississippi Bridge, King spotted the flashing light indicating for him to pull over.

"Pull over at the Highway Weight Station." The officer yelled on the loud speaker.

"Fuck!" Big Runn said, "We got all these fuckin' pistols in here!"

Calmly King said, "Just be cool."

The two officers got out of their car as one of them shouted on the loud speaker. "Driver, place both hands out the window."

King did as asked.

"Passenger, now place both of your hand out your window."

Ready for war, Runn did as he was asked.

"Now, you in the back seat, place your hands behind you head."

O refused. He slowly started to unzip his duffle bag and reached for his Glock. King glanced up in his rear view mirror and notice what his brother was about to do. He shook his head no.

Again the officer yelled out, "Sir! You in the back seat, put your hands behind your head."

"O, don't even think about it."

O stared at King with a smug look on his face, as he placed his hands behind his head.

With guns drawn the two officers walked toward the truck. One of the officers opened the back door, screaming "Step out of the truck now!"

O did as he was told.

"Keep your hands on top of your head and walk to the back of the truck, and place your hands on the truck."

The officer went into O's back pocket and got his I.D. and read it, "Lawrence Odom." He placed a pair of hand cuffs on him and told his partner, "We got 'em. It's him." Then, he walked O to the squad car and placed him in the back seat.

The other officer told King and Runn that they were free to go.

As they drove off, Runn sat in silence for a moment, then he asked. "Why in the hell didn't they search this truck? And why didn't you say something in the defense of your brother?" King looked straight ahead. Runn was puzzled. "You knew, didn't you? Those are a couple of your people, aren't they?"

King smiled, "Would you like to know? He didn't need to go with us no way. He would have gotten himself killed. I couldn't have that on my conscious. I promise to take care of him. He'll be alright until we make it back." King shook his head.

There was more going on that Runn didn't know. Those weren't his people; those where his sister, Keke's people. She hasn't always walked a straight and narrow path. Keke loved her brother but he was destroying the family. She called King late last night and told him that Lil Dillin passed and that she knew he was going after Black and that if he took O, she was afraid that he might come up dead too. She didn't want to lose another member of her family.

"So, they were your people?"

"Keke's. The officer that didn't say anything was Keke's ex. She called him while I was in Atlanta, and told him what was going on, and he promised her that he would do whatever she needed him to do."

"So she had him pick O up instead of someone killing him." Runn shook his head in dismay. "Y'all muthafuckas are too connected for me."

***

"Angie Wallace." the doctor said as she came out from the back.

"That's me." She looked Angie up and down before speaking. Moneeka notice the nervous look on her friend's face; sweat began to form on their forehead from anticipation. She handed Angie a pink piece of paper and walked off. Angie folded it up and shoved it in her right front pocket.

She couldn't bear to read the result at that moment. All she thought about was the young teen with the exact same form she was now holding.

"Come on, Ang." Moneeka said, "I'll take you home."

Upon exiting the clinic, Angie sat on the same bench as the teen. Lost in her train of thought, she didn't notice all the commotion in the middle of the street. People were running everywhere trying to get help. However, it was too late.

Angie and Moneeka walked to their car and looked at the accident and noticed that a body was covered up with a sheet.

"What happen?" Moneeka asked and older white woman.

"Poor child, just walked out in front of that 18 wheeler, with her head down, and he ran clean over her. Poor baby. They say she did it on purpose. They say she found out she had aids. But she read the paper wrong. It said for her to come back, it was a 50/50 chance if her partner had it. She was ok."

At that moment Moneeka looked at Angie and cried. They both had witness the girl crying and never said one word of comfort to her. They got in the car and drove off. Angie still wanted to be alone before she read it.

***

King and Runn entered St. Louis City limits. The sign board read "Welcome to St. Louis".

"Let's get in and out."

To Be Continued

Coming Soon!

B'Shone

ABOUT THE AUTHOR

B'SHONE, born and raised in Memphis TN attended Lincoln University and LeMoyn Owens College. He enjoys: singing and was once a member of the group 'Men-E-Faces'; swimming; and weight lifting is his favorite past time. He loves the Lord and the word of God.

Email him your comments and thoughts for the sequel, part two, 'The Evil Side of Her.

Email: Bshone72@yahoo.com

COMING SOON
By B'SHONE

The Evil Side of Her
Death Becomes Her
Playin' for Keeps
Deadly Consequences
Tangled Web of Love

B'Shone

www.ingramcontent.com/pod-product-compliance
Lightning Source LLC
Chambersburg PA
CBHW070119260626
47160CB00004B/1541